PENGUIN BOOKS
NO GOD IN SIGHT

Altaf Tyrewala lives in Bombay and Mumbai. He has worked as a
cashier, a telemarketer, a clerk and an instructional writer. This is his
first novel.

No God in Sight

ALTAF TYREWALA

PENGUIN BOOKS

PENGUIN BOOKS

Published by the Penguin Group

Penguin Books India Pvt. Ltd, 11 Community Centre, Panchsheel Park, New Delhi
110 017, India

Penguin Group (USA) Inc., 375 Hudson Street, New York, New York 10014, USA

Penguin Group (Canada), 90 Eglinton Avenue East, Suite 700, Toronto, Ontario,
M4P 2Y3, Canada (a division of Pearson Penguin Canada Inc.)

Penguin Books Ltd, 80 Strand, London WC2R 0RL, England

Penguin Ireland, 25 St Stephen's Green, Dublin 2, Ireland (a division of Penguin
Books Ltd)

Penguin Group (Australia), 250 Camberwell Road, Camberwell, Victoria 3124,
Australia (a division of Pearson Australia Group Pty Ltd)

Penguin Group (NZ), cnr Airborne and Rosedale Roads, Albany, Auckland 1310,
New Zealand (a division of Pearson New Zealand Ltd)

Penguin Group (South Africa) (Pty) Ltd, 24 Sturdee Avenue, Rosebank, Johannesburg
2196, South Africa

Penguin Books Ltd, Registered Offices: 80 Strand, London WC2R 0RL, England

First published by Penguin Books India 2005

Copyright © Altaf Tyrewala 2005

ISBN-13: 978-0-14400-060-9   ISBN-10: 0-14400-060-1

Typeset in Bembo by Mantra Virtual Services, New Delhi
Printed at Anubha Printers, Noida

no god in sight

Mrs Khwaja

I used to be a poetess and would dwell on minute metaphors for days.

Now all day long I cook for Ubaid and Minaz, spend the thousands their father earns every month, and contemplate television absent-mindedly.

I have nothing more to say.

The hum of air-conditioned rooms and twenty-four-hour TV has silenced me.

Mr Khwaja

Twenty-six years ago I married a mediocre poetess. She gave me two kids—a son who spends every waking hour online, and a daughter who's never home.

We live together and are still married, the woman and I.

The poetry has escaped our lives. I don't know her any more.

Ubaid

Home is where mom chases me with a plateful of food and frozen poems in her eyes. Where dad is vocal with his disapproval and where my sister Minaz, on witnessing the scenes, runs out the door like an anxious squirrel.

My heart isn't at home.

All day long I roam desolate cyber landscapes and chat with disembodied strangers—in search of a home, a heart.

Minaz

I won't be pregnant for too long now.

After we park the car near Colaba Post Office, my 'friend' and I walk to Pasta Lane under the severe afternoon sun. I spot Shamma Nursing Home on the ground floor of a decrepit building.

'We're here,' I say, and push open the clinic's door. Kasim doesn't follow me in. I come out to the footpath and give him my trademark tough stare—the look that has everyone fooled.

'Okay?' Kasim asks. I snort.

In a tasteless display of chivalry, he lets me enter first into the nursing home's dimly lit waiting room. It has the stench of a chloroform brewery.

A man is gazing at the frosted pane of a closed window. There is no one else in the room. Distracted by our entry, the man turns to look at us.

I can hear the gurgling in Kasim's throat as he struggles to frame a sentence. He seems confused. He appears to have forgotten why we are here.

'You…you are the doctor?' Kasim finally asks.

I snort again.

The doctor nods. He removes a sheet of paper from a desk-drawer and holds it out. *Which one of you wants this done most,* his action implies. I hum my assent and take the sheet. It is a form.

Ipshita never mentioned any freaking form! I widen my eyes at Kasim. He thinks I am asking for a pen and extends one in my direction. 'Take.'

It's a form, I mime wordlessly.

Kasim shrugs, *Just fill it.*

Are you mad?

Come on!

No. I throw the form on the doctor's desk and turn around and collide, violently and breast-to-breast, with a woman in a white sari.

Her type exists in every clinic. Nurses.

'Can't stand little far away!' I say.

The nurse prevents me from walking past her. 'Where you going? Why you acting so shy?'

'Just shut up!' I snap.

She grabs my arm. I look to Kasim for assistance.

'It's just a form,' the nurse says.

I struggle to free myself. 'Kasim…' I squirm. 'Kasim… Kasim…'

'Come, I'll fill it for you,' the nurse says. Still gripping my arm tightly, she unsheathes a ball pen from her immense blouse. 'Name?' she asks, bending over the form on the doctor's desk.

'O-madam, *name?*' the nurse looks up and repeats.

'Deepti,' Kasim says.

I stop struggling. Deepti. Deepti. Deepti. Deepti.

'Age?'

'Twenty-five,' he says.

'Your wife?'

Kasim gulps. Unlike me, he doesn't look a day older than his age of twenty. The nurse flares her nostrils sarcastically.

The doctor places before us an unmarked receipt for three hundred rupees. Kasim reaches for his wallet. I make a limp attempt to yank his hand from his back pocket. '*Just let me, okay*,' he whispers and reaches for his wallet again. He hands the doctor six fifty-rupee notes.

The doctor locks the entrance to the nursing home. He nods at the nurse. She lets go of my arm and follows her boss into the adjoining room, leaving Kasim and me by ourselves.

We stand like strangers in line for movie tickets.

I wish...

No, nothing. I don't wish anything.

'O-madam, you can come in now!' the nurse calls out moments later. Kasim practically tears through his pant pockets. Such urgency. And his cellphone isn't even ringing.

He brings it out and starts punching keys frantically.

The nurse reappears. 'Aye! You want to wait nine more months or what?'

Kasim stops punching. He doesn't look up. He just stands there, looking down at his cellphone.

I touch his elbow. 'Listen, if something goes wrong, just don't call my parents, okay?'

Then I leave him with his Nokia pacifier and follow the nurse into a hot, unventilated room.

The doctor seals its doors behind me.

The Doctor

I am an abortionist. I run a nursing home in a seedy by-lane of
Colaba. On the steely innards of trains crawling along the
Harbour Line, you will find badly spelt fliers advertising my
services. I get one or two customers every day. Sad cases, angry
faces, embarrassed women, careless men, swelling tummies, a
cut, tears, and we all go home happy. Yes, happy. I spread relief.
I save families, lives, marriages.

Now I need to be saved—from all the unborn-baby voices
in my head.

This afternoon a client walked into my nursing home with
her companion. Her stomach had just started to stick out. I
could see through her expensive cotton T-shirt. Three more
weeks and it would have been obvious. But she was safe now. I
handed her a form asking for personal information. The nurse
filled it out for her and handed it back to me. I don't talk to my
clients. I don't bother to read the forms either. They always lie.

I locked the entrance to my nursing home and nodded at
the nurse. We went into the adjoining room to prepare for the
operation. It was over in half an hour. Don't. Don't ask me about
the foetuses. They stopped registering after the third abortion.
Now, I only see them as knots of blood and gore. Abdominal
tumours that threaten to wreck the lives of decent, god-fearing
people.

I am married. She has the mentality of a farmer. Won't let me touch her willingly. I am violent with her every night. She says she won't give herself to me willingly till I stop harvesting the wombs of mothers. She even has the rhetoric of a farmer. If only my wife could see the gratitude in my clients' eyes. Like the girl this afternoon, the one in the expensive cotton T-shirt. She kissed my hand before I administered the anaesthesia. When she regained consciousness she wanted to know if it was a boy or a girl, she wanted to know if it was fair or dark, she wanted to know if it was normal or deformed, she wanted to know…'Or is it too early to tell? Can you tell? This soon? Tell me doctor! Am I right? Can you tell this soon?'

I didn't answer her. I don't talk to my clients.

I too will have a child someday. I will have several children, several. The collective cries of my children will hopefully drown out the unborn-baby voices in my head.

This is how my flier reads. Yes, it is badly spelt, unimaginative, but it gets the message across:

GET RID OF UNWANTED PREGNUNCY IN 1 HOUR
RUPEE 300 ABSOLUTELY SECRATIVE
SHAMMA NURSING HOME
OPP. JANVI MANZIL (BAHIND COLABA POST OFICE)

I composed it. My 'nun' pun makes me burst into amused hiccups every time I spot one of my fliers in a train. It is the only comic relief in my life. The family dramas that are occasionally staged in my nursing home don't amuse me any more. Their horrible echoes don't die for days: Daughters pleading with incensed fathers, husbands kneeling before heartless wives, brides begging with misogynist mothers-in-law to overlook the damning sonogram.

I have read that in America abortion is a source of perennial controversy. If you are 'pro' you are a murderer, cruel, careless. If you are 'anti' you are stupid, religious, but still careless.

I am neither.

And I am never careless. You can be either qualified or careful. I am very, very careful. That is why I get repeat business. Mostly from slim, college-going girls. There was one who visited me six times in two years. I haven't seen her for three years, now; doubt if I ever will again. Also, married women with their husbands. The first time is shameful and painful. The second time on, a routine sets in. Like visiting a dentist to fill a recurring cavity in a sweet tooth.

In a wilful attempt to decay and self-destruct, I have started smoking. Never in the nursing home. Always on the street outside the entrance. I never carry matches or a lighter. Asking for a light is my only excuse to talk to others. Unfortunately, the only people in the by-lanes of Colaba are pimps or German tourists in search of Aryan India—they first want to know if you are Brahmin. The man next door, the one who owns a souvenir shop, doesn't talk to me. He is a Jain, the epitome of non-violence. Won't even eat potatoes because their extraction deprives and kills underground insects.

I am an abortionist, and a Muslim to boot.

I have grown used to people avoiding me. Friends and relatives have gradually forsaken me over the years. They avoid me at the mosque. My wife and I are invited to marriages only out of formality. Even then we are ignored. Treated like well-dressed gatecrashers who can't be ejected (because you never know), but are watched from a distance.

Two years ago, my mother went to Mecca for Haj. For my sake. Just before boarding her flight, right there in the crowded departure lounge, Ma had looked at a point about two feet above my head and said, 'Oh Allah, I am undertaking this journey to your home so you may forgive my son and cause a change of heart in him so he may stop taking lives of children and find a cleaner occupation so when he has a child of his own he can love the child with all his heart and realize what a wondrous thing it is to nurture life…'

When I am in an irreverent mood, I like to believe that Ma paid with her life for such convoluted appeals to Allah. She was trampled while rushing to stone the Satan's pillar during Haj.

Of all the physical metaphors that thrive under an otherwise abstract Islam, the Satan's pillar—Jamarah Al-Aqabah—is most potent. After trekking back to Mina from Muzdalifa on the morning of the fourth day, as per tradition, two million pilgrims made a dash towards the Satan's pillar. They all wanted to be the first to stone it.

A woman who had been with Ma told me that Ma ran the fastest that morning. She pushed at the burgeoning crowds the hardest. She cursed the devil the loudest. Like some hysterical lioness whose cub was being snatched away. But in that crowd, there were people far more desperate than Ma. People whose sons were worse than abortionists. They, too, wanted to vanquish the devil with all their might. Those very people—those wretched, god-fearing fathers and mothers of sinners—ran over Ma and pounded her body into the Holy Ground.

Of the three hundred Indians who had gone to perform Haj that year, Ma was the only one who died in the stampede. She, and three Nigerians. My father, my wife and I got the news a day later. By then, they had already buried Ma's two-dimensional remains on the outskirts of Mecca.

When I try to imagine how she died that day in the Holy City, I stop believing in Allah. But only for a short while. I can't afford to remain godless for too long. The only way I can hide from myself is by being religious—or delusional. Call it whatever the hell you want. Ma's voice is now a part of the unborn-baby voices in my head.

Noise.

'Buy the cassettes. For fuck's sake, man, I need the cash. My whole collection for a hundred rupees only. Come on, dude, buy the friggin' cassettes!'

I didn't say no. I had bought all five audio cassettes from the drunk American who had barged into my nursing home six months ago. I didn't ask what kind of music it was. I didn't care. I wanted him out of my nursing home. He was making my nervous customers (two women) even more nervous. This happens all the time: cash-starved foreign tourists randomly barge into business establishments in Colaba to sell their personal belongings.

After the women left, I examined the cassettes I had been forced to buy. They had bizarre covers with outlandish words printed on them: Nirvana, Radiohead, Secret Samadhi and so on. English music, unfortunately.

That was the last day of Ramazan. The next day was to be

Eid. I was to put on laundered clothes and go to the mosque for the morning namaaz. At the mosque no one was to give me the three hugs that Muslim men are meant to exchange on auspicious occasions. I was to come home with a dry mouth, jerk my wife out of her sleep, open the cabinet in my hall, insert one of the English cassettes into my old player, and rewind it all the way to the start. I was to depress the Play button.

I didn't know I was to rattle with sorrow for the next thirty minutes.

I did. Like a laboratory skeleton dangling in an earthquake, like a sceptic to whom a saint had revealed his sainthood, I shook and wept tearlessly. The music that bled from the speakers matched the cacophony of unborn-baby voices in my head—discordant and raw and numbing. It consisted of singular strands of guitars so exquisite that they unfolded your leaden heart inside out and scraped away the pain and rage coagulating on its inner walls.

But these singular strands weren't what overwhelmed me. Beauty had stopped seeming beautiful to me a long time ago. It was the collective din of ten, hundred, million strands of guitars playing together that made my body convulse and my gaze still. Afsana, my wife, stood in a corner of the hall and watched me. Side A reached its end and the speakers bled silence.

I haven't played any of those cassettes again. It was enough that I had come across an analogue to the unborn-baby voices. I wasn't going to allow a new cacophony to compete with them. It was the least I could do to keep alive the memory of my dead mother. I can still hear her voice sometimes amidst the uproar in my head.

And the least I can do for my father?

To let him be. He threw out Afsana and me the day Ma's death washed up on our jagged beach. Having never opposed my occupation until then, he had called me a sister-fucking abortionist and told us to vacate in an hour. My wife and I now live in a building nearby. I haven't spoken to my father since. He too works in Colaba; has been a salesman at a shoe shop for thirty years. I see him sometimes.

Kaka

I saw him this morning. From the time he arrived at Dockyard Road station till he got off the train at VT, I watched him. I lost him in the morning rush at VT. He is young and walks much faster than me. Had he looked around Dockyard Road or turned his head in the train or lingered at VT for a moment, he would have spotted me in the crowd—the old man in the corner, the one who fathered him. But my son didn't see me because he doesn't look for me. In the train, amidst noisy fellow passengers, Akbar stood still and quiet, gazing at his nursing home's flier pasted on the concave part of the compartment where the ceiling meets the wall. For the twenty minutes the train ride lasted, I gawked at him secretly, watching every eye-blink, every twitch of his jawbone. Akbar has grown slimmer. He looks somewhat like me, but mostly his features have gone on his mother. His lower lip was red as usual. He has a habit of chewing it till the blood clots and tiny bruises appear.

As Akbar studied the flier, his lips suddenly plunged into a fleeting smile. And for that brief moment, the lump in my throat disappeared.

When I reach the shoe shop it is not yet ten-thirty. Only Amin-bhai is there. The two salesmen are invariably late: they saunter in by eleven or eleven-fifteen, wearing bright shirts and ugly jeans, talking gaudily. I find Amin-bhai, the owner, praying as usual in front of the Aga Khan's photograph. Jutting from three walls of the shop are shelves and shelves of shoes, sandals, stilettos, sneakers and slippers. The fourth wall is the entrance. Beneath is the floor. Above is the false ceiling, and in its centre is a dark square hole. I climb on top of the sofa for the customers. I reach up into the hole in the ceiling and pull down the ladder. I climb its uneven steps everyday to get to my place up there, between the shop's false ceiling and real ceiling, the mezzanine, where boxes and boxes of footwear are stocked.

I have sat up there for thirty years.

I clamber into the mezzanine and pull up the ladder. With my legs still dangling into the shop below, I grope around for the switch. Thirty years and I haven't yet memorized the geography of the mezzanine. When I go home, I don't remember where the switch is or where the ladder rests after I pull it up. I only recall the heady smell of polished leather and brand new rubber soles. I don't remember my wife's face either, only her delicate smell.

Good thing the train wasn't too crowded this morning. My son could stand comfortably. I know how much he hates others touching him, but it is unavoidable in trains on the Harbour Line. Once, when the compartment was crowded and Akbar was around, I had slipped my hand past torsos of fellow travellers, grabbed the shirt of the man farthest from me, and given it a hard yank. I am short, and remained undiscovered in the packed train. The men in between got dragged towards me; their collective weight crushed me against the metal wall, forcing me to hang out the door. I didn't mind, and neither should they.

Does their work require precision? Do their livelihoods demand a calm mind? Then what right did they have to crowd around Akbar, forcing him to lean back in obvious discomfort? The man whose shirt I yanked was inconveniencing my son the most.

'Kaka, Woodland W71, size 6!' Malik, the salesman, shouts.

I usually sit cross-legged at the edge of the mezzanine and peer at the customers below. They don't realize I'm up here till one of the salesmen barks orders at me. When customers look up and see me, their eyes widen. Women adjust their clothes to conceal or downplay their cleavages. Men pat their hair furtively.

This morning I have been so lost in my thoughts that I haven't noticed the arrival of the two salesmen or of the customers. When Malik shouts at me, his customer looks up in horror. My startled eyes blunder past her upturned face to her low-cut blouse. 'Eek, so sick!' the girl shrieks and scrambles out of my range to the rear of the shop.

Malik looks up and sniggers, 'Kaka, I'll drag you down by your dick if you do that again. Didn't you hear: Woodland W71, size 6? Get moving!'

Malik is twenty-four, and I, the man he calls Kaka, am sixty-five.

I uncross my feet and leap into a squat, and like a prawn I scuttle across the floor of the mezzanine to the far end, where the women's Woodland shoes are kept. W71—'W' for women and design number 71. I pull out a size-6 box and lift the lid. My wife would have liked these shoes, close-toed and flat-soled, sensible through and through.

In her final years she stopped making sense and became a mad fool. When our son failed his final MBBS exam, my wife said, 'Take it again.' Out of the question. We had mortgaged all the jewellery in the house and I had borrowed two lakhs from Amin-bhai. Enough. The family couldn't afford a student any more. A week later, without her knowledge, Akbar and I paid a quack in Colaba the deposit for the women's clinic he ran. After saving enough to purchase a degree from the University, the so-called doctor was joining a respected polyclinic as a gynaecologist. My son, shamed and matured by his failure, quietly complied with what had come his way. He had studied enough to operate in that nursing home. We didn't tell my wife. Akbar would leave every morning and return late. For three days my wife wondered where he had started going. On the fourth day she insisted on knowing. 'He goes to work,' I told her.

'What? Our son has started working? Where?'

'In three days he has already earned six hundred rupees,' I said proudly.

'Where does he work?' my wife persisted.

'At a rented clinic near my shoe shop.'

'Doesn't even have a degree! What does he do there?'

'Abortions.'

'You old rascal! Are you playing with yourself up there?' Malik shouts again.

Too many thoughts! I replace the lid and scuttle back to the opening in the mezzanine floor. 'Malik, take!' I call out.

He stretches up for the shoebox. 'Kaka, if you take this long again I swear I'll tell Amin-bhai. Sitting up there like a sister-sleeping king. Come down, no! Deal with the customers!'

I can't protest Malik's behaviour. Places of work flatten all differences between people. Malik and I are equals in this shop.

When I told my wife about our son's new livelihood, her lips went white and she shook her head disbelievingly, chanting, 'Ya Allah! Ya Allah! Ya Allah!' I whacked her on the back; she had become hysterical. 'Stop this!' I screamed at her. 'Thank your Allah that Akbar has started earning! Better days are ahead!'

Religion killed my wife. We could have lived our futures as proud and comfortable parents. Instead, she was visited by paralysing worries of sin and all that no-good dogmatic claptrap. First she begged me to stop Akbar from going to the nursing home—she called it the satanic butcher house. Then she attacked our son and threatened him with horrible visions of afterlife; the poor boy turned religious but didn't stop going to work. After he married, she nagged and nagged our daughter-in-law who just kept quiet and stood by Akbar dutifully.

There is no Allah, no heaven, no hell. No life after death. No sense in wasting precious hours of life inside mosques and temples and churches. When the stomach buckles and the skin sizzles, money is the only god who can answer prayers. How to tell the idiots in the world this? How to have told the idiots in my family this?

'I want to go for Haj,' my wife declared one day. I lifted my hand to slap her; my son held it back with just one word: 'Never.' He arranged everything for her; he also paid the Haj Committee at Crawford Market five thousand rupees extra for a special seat on the trip. What a waste of time and money and life. A week after she left, our telephone rang like an alarm bell at six in the morning. Akbar and I, startled out of our sleep, charged towards the phone from opposite directions. I picked up the receiver and put it down two minutes later without saying a word. What was there to say? Who had sent her there? Who had encouraged her nonsense? And as the final, treacherous, cruel blow against my son in what was probably the darkest hour of his life, I demanded: Whose bastard livelihood had driven my wife to Mecca?

How he left home! A few angry words from me in that grief-stricken moment and he was off. As if he had been waiting to be offended so he could snap ties with the click of a suitcase and walk away in a huff. I wonder, do such people return? Can they come back and erase the paralysing dot-dot-dots in the lives of those they have left behind?

Akbar has his wife. She loves him fully and in time they will have children. He is not alone. The thought relieves me.

It is getting tougher to climb to the mezzanine; these knees have grown a mind of their own, sometimes pliant, sometimes resolutely unbendable. It is old age, of course, although my hair is still black and my teeth intact. It must be because of the dustless environment of the mezzanine; up here it is cool no matter what season reigns outside the shop. But beneath the sparsely wrinkled skin and black hair, this body is slowly and gradually winding up.

There is a closing-down sale in the shoe shop. Twenty to seventy per cent off. Amin-bhai wants to move to America with his wife and three-year-old twins. His father died years ago. It has been two months since his mother expired. Now Amin-bhai has no more ties to India. He says in America he will work at his elder brother's grocery store. He has generously excused my debts and asked that in return I pray he and his family get visas. Prospective buyers and estate agents have already begun visiting the shoe shop. No new wares are being ordered.

I stopped praying years ago. I'm not going to start now for Amin-bhai's visas.

Amin-bhai

Rukhshana and I had asked so many, many people to pray for us that I was certain when we arrived at the American embassy our visas would be awaiting us at the entrance. No waiting, no interview. Just a sealed envelope that said, *For the Bootwalas: Special Lifelong Visas Granted by Popular Demand to the Divine.*

Ya, right.

First we have to stand in line for three hours on the footpath outside the embassy. Then we have to sit for two more hours inside. And through all this I have to apologize for having ridiculed Rukhshana's mother's (ridiculous) suggestion that we camp all night outside the embassy.

Sometime close to afternoon, after I have exhausted myself imagining the worst possible scenarios, our names are announced on the sound system: 'Amin Bootwala and family, cubicle 7... Amin Bootwala and family...'

We gather our things and our wits together and get to our feet.

I follow my wife and twins into a tiny cubicle. It is cold and smells of mint, like the America I imagine. Behind a glass screen sits a stout foreigner. In a green shirt and grey tie he looks like a CNN anchor. For the first time since birth, my three-year-old twins don't fidget. We all stand dwarfed and paralysed in awe of the American embassy official—our saviour, our deliverer.

I hope he notes the subtle pinstripes on my five-thousand-rupee suit. I am not anxious about my wife's lakh-a-piece diamond earrings—they are impossible to ignore. But I hope the interviewer knows how expensive denim dungarees for three-year-olds can get.

'Hey,' the interviewer says. He is flipping through our forms and passports.

'How you doin'?' I ask. That's how American customers greet me at the shop.

Our interviewer looks up with raised eyebrows. 'Not bad,' he says, and looks down again.

A cold sweat breaks across my back. It is the first such moment since I graduated—when the rest of my life depended on the momentary whim of an unknown official correcting my papers or granting me admission. At least I can see this man's pasty face.

'So, Mr Amin Bootwala,' the American says, pronouncing my name like 'amen', 'your visa application says you own a shoe shop in Colaba…?' He trails off.

I want to talk and never stop. I want to recount our life histories so this embassy man will believe we are the good ones, the ones who will come back, not the type who will wind up working at some grocery store in New Jersey. The good ones. Rukhshana looks at me anxiously. I say, 'Right, sir, on Colaba Causeway. It's called True Shoe, established by my father forty years ago. We are very well-known…'

The interviewer looks at Rukhshana. 'And Mrs Bootwala, what do you do?'

'I'm a housewife. Kids, you know.' Rukhshana ruffles the hair on one of their heads.

The embassy man points at our forms. 'You say here you'll be visiting your friend in Seattle. Is that right?'

I start to speak, 'Uh yes, sir, that…'

But my reply is nipped by an Indian woman who enters from a door behind the interviewer.

She doesn't even look at us. 'Here you go, Steve!' She hands the American a sheet of paper and leaves.

He squints at it. And upon reading the contents of the sheet, our interviewer's face reddens; his thin lips virtually disappear. He looks up at us and presses the sheet against the glass screen. 'Man! Can you *believe* this?'

SHIT!

JUNAID!

They must have tracked his visa application from two years ago!

They must know my elder brother hasn't returned!

They will stamp 'Rejected Forever' on our passports and fling them at our faces.

I panic in the face of failure: 'I have all my documents, sir!' I hold up the folder. 'My bank statements, tax returns, property papers. All latest, all in order!'

Our interviewer frowns, 'What're you talking about?' Then he shivers the sheet impatiently and begins reading, 'Get a load a' this bull. Blah blah blah…embassy personnel are to observe regular working hours on Saturday 25th owing to vast task backlogs…blah blah blah…many thanks, sincerely…'

He looks up murderously. 'You tell me, Mr Bootwala, do I look like a machine?'

It's like God being facile on Judgement Day—you have to

go along without seeming slavish or impudent.

I stare like a nitwit.

'It's…it's very unfair for you?' Rukhshana offers with caution.

Our interviewer nods vigorously. 'Thank you, Mrs Bootwala! I mean, a six-day week? It's criminal! Like we don't work hard enough!'

I frown and smack my lips. Rukhshana purrs empathetically. The twins maintain a sensitive stillness. The American stamps four pink slips and slides them through an opening. They fall into a stainless-steel receptacle on our side.

'I'm tellin' ya,' he continues, stacking our passports like playing cards, 'if this was America, this embassy would a' been busted for malpractice.'

I stare at the pink slips.

'Go on, take the receipts, you got your six-month visas,' the American says. The simplicity of our success is stunning. 'Pay your money now and pick up your passports in the afternoon, all right?'

Rukhshana and I begin glutting him with thank-yous. He waves us out modestly.

'Hey, Bootwalas!' the American shouts after we step out. We stick our heads into the cubicle. 'You know where to find me this Saturday, right?' he roars.

We erupt into joyous, guttural laughter.

In the taxi, Rukhshana and I exchange grins over our twins' heads. We won't have to go to an immigration expert after all.

I look out the window, at the grey urban landscape whizzing by. The traffic feels comical now, the beggars seem charismatic in their wretchedness, fumes from trucks and buses tickle our sinuses, and when Hamid's asthma acts up like it always does— he was born with it—Rukhshana cuddles him and covers his face with her sari. 'Shh…'

Hhzzz. My son's wheezing struggles to be heard over the din of electric horns, old engines, bus bells and barking dogs. Farid clutches his brother's hand. 'Roll up the windows,' Rukhshana says. The taxi driver and I obey. Rukhshana rubs Hamid's tiny chest. The old anger returns. Hhzzz. Rukhshana and I exchange helpless glances. 'Shh…shh…' Hhzzz. Hhzzz. This dusty, dirty country. This dump of a subcontinent that will kill each one of us.

Hamid, exhausted by the attack, falls asleep. I extricate Farid's hand from his brother's death-like grip.

The taxi pulls up outside our colony. 'Take an off today?' Rukhshana tempts me. I hand her Hamid.

'Start packing, we'll fly as soon as possible.'

Rukhshana seems alarmed.

I close my eyes reassuringly. 'We'll manage.' I pat the taxi driver's shoulder. 'Let's go.'

In half an hour I am at the shoe shop. I stand outside on the footpath and look up at True Shoe, at the cream and black signboard, at the tinted glass entrance and the barely stocked shelves of footwear inside.

There are no customers. When I enter, Malik and Bhupendra, the two salesmen, don't stand up, they don't even stir. Since Kaka's death nine days ago, employee morale has plunged.

'How's business?'

'Cold,' Malik mumbles.

I sit in the leather chair behind the cash counter. The bill book indicates only one sale for the day. A pleasant surprise, actually, considering there's nothing in stock but outdated ladies' sandals, Hawaii chappals and kids' shoes.

I load two envelopes with three thousand rupees each. 'Get your bags,' I say.

Malik and Bhupendra remove their plastic bags from the closet. They come to the counter. I stand up to give them their last and final pays. They don't ask unnecessary questions. Did I get my visa? When am I leaving? My salesmen are smart. I was worried for Kaka, but he, like everything else, is now a closed chapter, finished and done under six feet of fertile graveyard grime.

'Best of luck, Amin-bhai,' Bhupendra says.

'Ya-ali-madad, Amin-bhai,' Malik says as he follows his colleague through the door.

'Mowla-ali-madad,' I say. 'Down the shutter half!'

Malik nods.

And probably for the first time in forty years the shutter of True Shoe stands at half mast at three in the afternoon on a normal, working, non-holiday.

Here's how it will happen:

I will telephone Mr Lakhani.

Before sunset he will arrive at the shop with a briefcase containing money and I will sign away this 300 sq. ft., forty-year-old institution of sorts for fifty-three lakh rupees, seven lakhs below its market value.

The house will be in a mess when I return. The kids will be

at the neighbour's. Rukhshana will be hyperventilating over all the things that need packing, all the things that need salvaging, saving, stowing. I will seat her on the bed. I will place my hands on her shoulders and tell her to take just our clothes, that's it, only our clothes.

A week later—after seven days of shopping, discarding and disconnecting—my wife, my two children and I will come out of our flat for what I hope will be the last time in our lives. The time will be nine p.m. We will have five whole hours to go before take-off. I will padlock the main door to the house; we will already have sealed its windows and switched off its electric main.

We will haul five suitcases into the back of and atop the roof of a taxi. My carryall will contain photographs of my parents, Rukhshana's parents, and of our vacations—first as a couple and then as a family.

On our way to the airport we will keep the windows up.

We will become worried and impatient in the long check-in line. The police will question us. Passport officials will question us. I will answer patiently. I may even smile.

And finally we will have finished with all formalities. We will haul our hand luggage and our children towards the departure lounge.

Two hours later we will board the plane. And my children, like children are wont to before take-off, will start crying, screaming, bawling. Other children will join in like members of a sullen choir.

Below the howl of take-off, the city of our birth—the nation of our ancestors—will fade into a twinkling sprawl of lights and then into a distant flicker and then it will be gone, gobbled and blackened by distance. *It wasn't worth it*, I will tell myself. And I will repeat, like a mantra, like a dua, *it wasn't worth it, it wasn't worth it.* And even then, if my idiot nostalgia refuses to die, I will remember the protection money demanded, the covert and blatant religious slurs, the riots, the aftermaths, the newborn niece named Nidhi, the rewritten history books, the harassment at the passport office. Wasn't it enough, wasn't it enough that we lived in our ghettos and worked in our holes and paid our taxes and demanded nothing in return?

The aircraft's projection screen will show a blue India, with our plane's route-so-far outlined in white like an anaemic tapeworm in the belly of a diseased nation.

I will sit back in my seat and pretend to breathe easy. *Forget it,* I will tell myself, *let go.* Let them have it, let them have what they have killed clergymen for, razed mosques for, driven out fellow Indians for.

Let them have their Hindustan for Hindus.

the very beginning

Babua

Namaste. My name is Babua. I live in Barauli, a village like any other village.

Today is my sixteenth birthday.

It is mid-morning. I am napping on a charpoy under a hay shack located on the outer edge of my father's orchard. I hear a lascivious giggle. I open my eyes and find Lajwanti, the most recent addition to our gaggle of village nymphos, lolling against one of the poles. She is wearing a yellow skirt and a red come-hither blouse. 'What you want?' I say.

'Aye, take me rey,' she says.

Lajwanti is a worker's daughter. I am overjoyed that I, the landlord's son, have been included in this working-class sweet-sixteen deflowering tradition. Truly, there is nothing more democratic than sex. 'Let's go!' I say.

I follow Lajwanti into the cornfields. She stretches out in a clearing. I remove pertinent items of my clothing. Lajwanti parts pertinent segments of her anatomy. Then she waits and waits. 'What's wrong?' she says.

I don't know! I am trying my best!

'Thoo-thoo!' Lajwanti says. She stands up, dusts her clothes and skips off, giggling cruelly.

I lie there in a corny, horny daze.

That's right: my very first chance to khutt-khutt and my

tools have failed me. I can't believe it!

After the Lajwanti disaster I think about running away to escape the dishonour. Thankfully, she runs away first—to become an actress.

Lajwanti's departure means my secret is safe. But my problem persists. I start peeping into my dhoti several times a day, praying, hoping and begging for something to happen.

After that day in the fields I read no books, watch no serials and hear no music. My days begin and end obsessing over the morgue in my dhoti.

A year later, I turn seventeen.

'You are a man now, Babua!' father announces.

'You are old enough to shoulder my corpse!' grandfather says with his characteristic morbidity.

I am hoping my sires' baritones will impress my necropolis. Alas, my tools are deader and deafer than I thought. Nothing stirs.

Then, one afternoon, after gazing at my jewels for many, many hours, the error of my ways smacks me on the head. I fasten my dhoti. What eggs hatch when watched, haanh? I realize I have to find something else to do. I have to think of anything other than...

So I go looking for father and find him hunched over a sapling in our orchard. 'Give me something to do,' I say.

'There is nothing to do,' father looks up and replies. He sweeps his hand over our huge orchard crammed with workers and trees, 'I have worked hard, so your sons and your sons' sons don't have to lift a finger. Just relax, Babua.'

I squat beside father. 'You don't understand. I can't have sons if I don't do anything.'

He is aghast. 'What do you mean? You will marry a woman, then you will have children…'

I make a face. 'It's not that simple, okay!'

Father cries, 'It is! You are a man just like me and your grandfather!'

I ask, 'Why?'

Father replies, '*Why*? What *why*? Be gone, Babua, your questions aggravate me.'

I stand up. 'A nice way to dismiss a man, haanh, Baba?' I deliver my parting shot and return to the spot behind the well to look inside my dhoti.

What should I do? Oho-rey, I cry to myself, *what should I do?* I want to be a man like my grandfather; a man like my father, whose rare words and ample riches make people tremble. I want to be like the barber, doctor, bus driver, and even our orchard workers—they are all men, siring sons like rabbits, unmindful of their bodies.

Mahant Suyansh would say, *Men must fulfil their dharma.*

I don't have any dharma. Mahant Suyansh, on the other hand, has loads of it. He is our local sage and seer. On his monthly visits to Barauli, he mounts a chair on our porch, furls in his saffron robes and addresses the villagers. The Mahant's discourses are unintelligible. But we are all mesmerized by his immersion. Once, to demonstrate the mythical marriage of some god with some goddess, the Mahant had stabbed his thumb and smeared blood on his widow's peak; the details I never did catch, but I will never forget the blood trickling down his forehead.

The Mahant certainly doesn't waste a moment pondering over his lungi, leave alone what is inside it. Like my ascendants he, too, is a man. Religion and mythos are his wards and he injures himself in their upkeep.

So, am I to remain half a man till I have inherited the orchard? Till I have remained engrossed for hours like father in the selection of manure, am I to think of nothing but my giraffe that won't lift its neck? Inside my wide chest is an ant's heart, and in this heart is immense regret for having a lineage that, by giving me everything, has left me with nothing better to do than contemplate the catastrophe in my dhoti.

Then, one afternoon (funny how all the important stuff happens in the afternoon), as I am napping in my room, I hear my mother scream, 'Babua!'

I hear a commotion outside. I panic. 'What–what?' I fasten my dhoti and run out of my room. 'What happened?' There are several villagers in the veranda. More are gathering by the second.

'The Mahant!' mother screams. 'The Mahant is coming!'

Again? A second visit to Barauli in the same month? This is extraordinary!

'Start preparing!' I shout.

Minutes later, the Mahant hurries in through our gate. Work stops with unprecedented swiftness: the bus driver abandons his vehicle mid-road, women kill the flames under half-boiled pots of rice, and everyone rushes to our courtyard within minutes of the Mahant's arrival.

He refuses lunch and damn near hurts himself in his scramble to mount his seat.

I sit next to father at the foot of the Mahant's chair—my new position since turning seventeen—and look down at my dhoti, as usual.

The Mahant raises his hands. The crowd becomes quiet.

'Eunuchs!' the Mahant screeches, half-leaping off his chair, sending his saffron robes pell-mell. His angry finger sweeps over the hushed crowd. 'Moustaches and dhotis. If you have wives also, so what? Eunuchs! All! Eunuchs! You are all eunuchs!'

The Mahant claps his hands. His spittle descends on father and me like a foul mist. I am astonished by the god-man's vulgar clarity. Gone are the tales of scorpion gods and nebulous universes. For the first time there is no mistaking the Mahant's discourse.

He is talking to me!

'Your safes. Keep them open. Your women's legs. Keep them parted. Right now, lambs and goats. The outsiders are sharpening knives on animals. One day, it will be your necks. Your women. Your money. Hai-hai, sixers! Who is not eunuch here? By their beards, grab the outsiders. Out. Throw them out. Which man will do it? Throw out the outsiders from your house, your village, your country. Hindustan for Hindus! Hindustan for Hindus! Understand, donkey eunuchs? Not for outsiders, our Hindustan! Who? Who will correct history, who will avenge the past and drive the outsiders out…?'

Zail Singh, the Scapegoat

I am standing at the back of the crowd, enjoying the drama. All of a sudden Babua, who is sitting beside his father at the foot of the Mahant's chair, jumps up and says, 'I will do it, Mahant. I am not a eunuch! I will drive out the outsiders!'

The Mahant thumps Babua on the shoulder. 'Here is a man! Go! Throw them out!'

Babua tightens his dhoti. Then he touches the Mahant's feet, bows to his father, and descends the steps of their porch. He stands before the crowd and looks us over like a policeman trying to decide who is guilty.

I disguise my laugh with a cough. Such fun! Just like cinema!

Babua approaches the squatting villagers. They move their legs and lean to the right and left to let the youth through. The Mahant raises his hands and shouts at the sky. 'Go forth, oh son of Hindustan for Hindus! By their beards, grab them. Yours it is—Hindustan. From the outsiders reclaim it!'

Babua doesn't walk; he prowls. With every step, his back straightens and his chest inflates like a dolly being pumped through its nozzle.

Oye. Too funny. 'Uhhoo, uhhoo!' I cover my mouth and cough with uncontrollable mirth.

The people standing around look at me distractedly. Babua notices the faces turning in my direction. The seated villagers, noting Babua's frozen stare, swivel their heads. I look around.

Babua, and everyone else, is looking at me.

What the fuck!

Babua comes and stands before me. 'Hello, Babua,' I say, nodding respectfully, biting my tongue to stop the laughter. He is a whole head shorter.

'Hindustan for Hindus!' Babua shrieks into my face. He grabs my beard. It feels like needles poking out from inside my jaw.

'Abbey! Let go!' I shout, and catch Babua's hand.

'Hindustan for Hindus!' he shrieks again.

The pain blackens my sight. I flail weakly in Babua's grip as he drags me by my beard to the Mahant.

An Omniscient Villager

Yaar. The Sikh got screwed.

When Babua dragged Zail Singh to the front, the Mahant took one look and hopped upon his chair. 'You eunuch! Donkey! Leave it! Leave his beard!'

Babua hung on in puzzlement. Zail Singh lifted his hand with considerable effort and boxed Babua's ear. Babua fell to the right; Zail Singh collapsed to the left, massaging his jaw and moaning in pain, 'Maadar da phaataa, saala, todi ma di aankh!'

Perched on the chair, the Mahant began clapping like mad. 'You eunuch! Sixer! Go attack real outsiders!'

Babua stood up rubbing his head. He argued petulantly, 'This Zail Singh is not from our village. He has beard. He is outsider. He is!'

The Mahant hollered, 'Sixer! He is Sikh. Not outsider! Sikh is Hindu!'

Zail Singh heaved and got to his feet. 'Oye, I'm not Hindu, I'm Sikh, not Hindu, and I'm going back to Karnala right now.' He walked away, muttering, muttering.

Babua scanned the crowd with growing shame. He turned to the Mahant. 'Tell me, Mahant, who you want me to throw out? Who is the outsider? You tell me, I will throw him out right now in front of you. I am not eunuch!' Then he screamed desperately, 'Hindustan for Hindus!'

The Mahant didn't answer; he placed his hands on his head and looked down in resignation. Someone at the back started giggling. The laughter spread like plague. Villagers were falling over each other for support. Babua ran into his house, inflamed with hate for an outsider he didn't even know.

Over subsequent days, the people of Barauli re-enacted the fiasco repeatedly. Someone would impersonate the Mahant, another would ask to play Babua, and several would vie for Zail Singh's role. Over several replays, hyperbole morphed the original event into something else entirely: after a lewd dispute over pubic hair, an incensed Zail Singh would thrash a stone-blind Babua and chase away a high-strung Mahant.

Not all the villagers ran to watch and cheer these performances.

There were a few who merely chuckled with indulgence at these impromptu skits and continued with their tasks. The sudden reticence of these few went unobserved. No one noticed that their businesses were opening late and closing early. That the stocks in their shops and workshops weren't being replenished. That the men amongst these few went on mysterious trips with their wives and children, carrying trunks and cartons, and that these men returned next day empty-handed and alone. The withdrawal of these few was like the invisible dwindling of an invalid. When they were all finally gone, no one in the village even noticed.

And then it was too late. A month later, the Mahant reappeared with eighty men. They poked the air above their heads with tridents. The motley crew kicked up dust and startled birds with roars of 'Hindustan for Hindus! Out with outsiders!'

Seeing that the Mahant was responsible for this early morning ruckus, the villagers calmed down and squatted outside their homes. They looked forward to another juicy farce and one more vain witch-hunt for an outsider who just didn't exist here, in this village, where everyone knew everyone.

The Mahant and his men broke into seven cottages. They forced up the shutters to five workshops and two shops. Bare walls and cupboards were all they found.

The mob rushed to the west of the village. Without removing their shoes, they barged into a structure where people once prayed.

'Empty. All of it. Fled. All of them,' the Mahant spat at his disappointed eighty.

Babua had come rushing, enthused with anger towards an outsider he would finally discover.

Hanging around the edge of the Mahant's herd, Babua was now doubly unsure why the outsiders were who they were.

Suleiman, the Outsider

I get off the train at Namnagar and trudge to my great-grandfather's house two streets from the station. Who am I? Where have I come from? Why am I in Namnagar, carting my life's possessions like a refugee?

I don't have time to explain.

I knock on the light blue, flaking door. Shazia-dadi, my septuagenarian spinster grand-aunt, opens the door and encircles me in arms gnarled like branches. 'Suleiman, I haven't seen you in two years. How you've grown!' she cackles.

'No one grows at twenty-seven,' I say.

I drop my four bags and dart around the house looking for him. 'Where is he?' (I have no name for great-grandpa.)

'Abbu's sleeping,' Shazia-dadi says.

'At one in the afternoon?'

'Abbu's ninety-six. He can sleep for ever,' Shazia-dadi remarks with awe.

'Wake him,' I say, and begin walking in and out of rooms to find him. Shazia-dadi follows me around like a chick, cheeping her protestations. I raise my voice: 'Tell me! Where is he?'

Flaunting a wet, gummy smile, she points to a room I had just inspected. 'Heeheehee. You missed Abbu. He's in there.'

I rush back in. Great-grandpa has shrunk. Not only in length and breadth; his width is under attack. He is lying on his back, flat as the mattress. I go up to his bed below a curtained window and shake his bony arm. Dadi pats her cheek to warn me of the slap I will receive for this insolence. Is she still afraid of her father? This withering husk of a thing?

I stoop to his ear and whisper in a voice made hoarse by thirst and dust, 'Come on, wake up. I have to ask you something.' It is vile to do this to a man this ancient, but had my father, a carpenter, been alive, he would have been rougher.

Great-grandpa flutters his eyelids. I prop him up on a pillow and give him water.

'Remember your son Allaudin?' I ask.

Great-grandpa stops sipping and raises his head in distress. 'Allaudin, my peace of heart! Why Allah didn't take me instead!'

'Okay, okay. You remember Allaudin's son, Nizar?' I ask.

He stops sipping again. 'Nizar, my grandson, how I miss him! Why Allah didn't take me instead!'

I snatch the glass from his hands. 'I am Nizar's son. My name is Suleiman. Do you remember?'

Facts tear through great-grandpa's senility. His eyes dilate with recognition. 'Suleiman, poor orphan, both parents dead. But don't worry, I am still here, your great-grandfather.' He strains forward and taps my hand. Shazia-dadi pats my shoulder. The ambitious kindness of feeble kin. I am nearly tempted to skip what I have come for. But it has to be done.

Softening my tone, I proceed carefully. 'Do you know what has happened?' I lean closer to great-grandpa. 'They drove out all Muslims from Barauli, my village. The Mahant said we are outsiders. We have abandoned our houses and shops and some have fled to Bombay, some to Hyderabad.'

Great-grandpa says in his scratchy voice, 'Suleiman, you live here with us. You are a carpenter, no? You can begin afresh in Namnagar.'

'No,' I hiss like a boa, 'I am not a carpenter. My father was a carpenter. I am a tailor, and I too am going to Bombay to live like other refugees…'

Great-grandpa's jaw drops with exhaustion.

I continue with a colossal pretence of calm, 'But before I go, I must understand. I must know so I can endure. Only you can tell me because *you*, *you* severed us from who we were, *you* turned us into outsiders to be driven out of villages…'

(Shazia-dadi pokes my shoulder. But today nothing is going to stop me.)

'So, now tell me,' I say. 'Why? Why did you convert?'

(Shazia-dadi yelps.)

'Haanh? What came over you? What mischief made you become a bloody Muslim?'

The Convert

Suleiman's question knocks the wind out of me.

When I reopen my eyes hours later, it is night. The bulb in my room burns weaker than ever. In an irrelevant hamlet like Namnagar, even our electricity seems to lack confidence. Except for a circle of light to the left of my bed, the room is dark. Suleiman and my daughter Shazia are talking in the adjoining room. I am gladdened to hear the accompanying clatter of silverware. That even today, at my age, my children eat what I provide is an excellent compliment.

Be it taxes, obligations, or misery, I have never evaded anything. When I passed out on hearing Suleiman's question, I wasn't taking refuge in sleep. I was revisiting the past. I have picked out the necessary facts and reasons from its huge storeroom and am ready to answer my great-grandson's question: *Why did I become a Muslim?* But, before I answer, I too have a question to ask Suleiman: *How does it matter?*

If he isn't silenced by my counter-query, I will doze off again. I will sleep till my great-grandson tires of waiting and goes away. Regardless of my reply, Suleiman will remain a Muslim and must survive the trials of these times. Asking a ninety-six-year-old man why he did what he did seventy years ago isn't a solution to anything. What will Suleiman do with my answer? Sing it in trains? And what if even that doesn't work? Will he then change his name to Suresh, shave his beard, and stop going to the mosque? It is futile. And so I will sleep.

I used to think old people sleep to rest. It was so till about six years ago. Sometime during my ninetieth year, my sores and fevers ceased to torment me. They are still there, I'm sure; the doctor visits every week to fuss over them. But now, when I moan during the medico's poking and prodding or when I grunt as Shazia attempts to feed and clean me, it isn't pain I am bewailing. All I want to do is sleep. If you can call it that. Unlike the coma of youth, when yesterday, today and tomorrow cross-bred to spin visions of infinite hues and moods, my sleep is dreamless. I used to think old people relive memories in tedious detail. That may be true of the moment of death. I, for one, can conjure and dismiss my yesterdays like so many measly genies. In my sleep I go nowhere, regret nothing, and miss no one, like sitting in an empty darkened theatre staring at a blank screen.

Morning must be approaching. When I open my eyes again, the room seems brighter than before. Why doesn't Shazia turn off the bulb? She knows we can't afford to burn power without reason.

Suleiman is sitting next to me, on my bed, watching over me like a vulture. He sees me stirring and jumps at the opportunity. 'Tell me, please! Why? Why did you convert? Why did you become a Muslim?'

I do everything it takes to smile, but my lips don't obey. I close my eyes again, to shut out the glare of Suleiman's stare.

He seems old enough to have questioned—if youngsters still do it—life. To have contemplated his own existence and the existence of an Almighty. Or maybe not. Men like my great-grandson, born into a pervasive monolith of a faith, have little reason to be inquisitive or anxious. When a holy book provides answers before you have questioned, and your day is neatly partitioned into five prayer sessions before you are born, you would have to be a fool, or an innately disruptive person, to nurse doubt. Oh, but the nobility of questioning customs, suspecting idols and searching for years! And the thrill of finding your answers in a holy book! And the comfort in having your previously formless days neatly partitioned into sessions of five! Suleiman will never know such delight and I pity him for it.

It is Shazia's delicate touch on my shoulder. 'Abbu. Abbu, wake up. Time for dinner,' she whispers.

It is daylight now. A mellow, velvety morning.

'Turn off the light, damn hell!' I say.

Suleiman, with food-tray in hand, turns to look at the glowing bulb. 'Come on, Abbu,' Shazia says, 'if I switch off the bulb, how will I see you, hmm? See what's for dinner, you'll love what I made.' She tries to prop me up.

I start to tell my loving but foolish daughter that it's morning, time to turn off the bulb and feed me breakfast, not dinner. But I don't say it.

The truth…the truth of the moment…the truth of the moment whisks my words away.

Hey Ram. Ram-Ram.

As I breathe my last, I hope Suleiman doesn't think his question was the death of me.

Shazia-dadi, the Genius

Suleiman thought his question was the death of Abbu.

He rested his head on Abbu's arm and wept. I stroked his head and pacified him with kissing sounds.

I am cursed. At the most delicate of moments my thoughts are invariably profane. Abbu is dead. No point describing how cleaning and changing him twice a day—*my own father!*—would spark thoughts that embarrass me. Stroking Suleiman's head, I imagined how pleasurable it would be to...oh, sick. Even at seventy-one every man seems a potential. Reason must intervene on every occasion and prompt my virginal subconscious in a hushed murmur: he is father, he is brother, he is milkman, he is postman...Suleiman is my brother's son's son. My grandson. *My grandson!* I repeated it several times till the feel of his coarse hair turned indistinguishable from that of any other object.

'Son,' I said at last with complete conviction, 'we must arrange his funeral.'

Suleiman raised his wet, grieving face, 'My question distressed him, Shazia-dadi. I killed him. I killed him!'

At Abbu's age, so much as a gentle breeze could have polished him off. But I didn't tell Suleiman that. His guilt was precious to me.

At birth, marriage and death, a man's life isn't his own. Abbu's funeral was a circus. While washing Abbu's corpse, the maulvi dropped it in alarm. 'Oh, the profanity, the deceased is uncut!'

Uncut? Uncut. *Uncut?* Yes, yes, uncut!

The question and answer crept through the acquaintances who had gathered at the graveyard. What was uncut? No one would tell me. I sat alone on the special spot for females near the entrance. 'He's a convert, maybe that's why?' Suleiman suggested to the maulvi.

A convert? A convert. *A convert?* Yes, yes, a convert!

Another round of whispered gossip. Another maulvi stepped in and finished what the earlier one had abandoned in horror.

The following week blurred by.

Then the day came: the day of Suleiman's departure.

I began by saying, 'Been just nine days since Abbu. Stay some more, Suleiman.'

Didn't work.

So I asked, 'Why be a refugee in an unknown city? This house is yours only.'

No effect.

So I cried, 'Stay! Have pity on a seventy-plus woman!'

Suleiman continued to pack with a chilling apathy. This was the world Abbu said he would always shield me from: a world uncaring of a woman who had never married or bred. But to be treated like this by one of your own? 'Oh, Abbu!' I gasped, lamenting his absence and the profound loneliness that lay ahead.

'What's that?' Suleiman looked up from a bag he was bending over.

'You killed my Abbu,' I whispered. This was my desperation

talking. Suleiman froze. 'Your anger, your question, it crushed my frail old father.' Suleiman hid his face in his hands. I concluded with a curse, like a haggard second-rate witch: 'Wherever you go, whatever you do, never forget that you stripped a lonely old woman of her one and last protector.'

Suleiman looked up with the same wet grieving face he had at Abbu's death. 'But I can't stay here, dadi! I can't! The woman I love is waiting for me in Mumbai!'

'Then take me along!' I joined my hands and begged. 'As your mother, as your responsibility, you must take me with you to Mumbai!'

Abbu would have been happy to know: For the first time I left a man speechless and unable to say 'no'.

Nilofer, the Martyr

Trust Suleiman to set off alone and return with a bent old woman in tow. I was in our tin shack, resigned to sleeping alone for the ninth night in this alien city, when Suleiman appeared at our joke of a door. 'Nilofer, I'm back!'

'You took so long coming!' I whined. From Barauli station I had come to Mumbai with my uncle, while Suleiman had gone to Namnagar. I leaned forward to embrace him. Suleiman raised his eyebrows in warning. I reached for his mouth. He averted his face. *No, no*, he mimed. 'Why not, dear?' I peered over his shoulder and literally leapt off Suleiman for decency's sake.

'Who's she?' I inquired softly.

So.

Shazia-dadi didn't like our ten-by-ten tin shack; too tinny and suffocating she said. She hated the curtain we drew across the room for privacy. She loathed the two loos shared by nine other slum-dwelling families. And she *refused* to digest the food I made, and the fact that Suleiman and I lived in sin. We are orphans. Except for my uncle who couldn't care less and Shazia-dadi who was too new to matter, Suleiman and I had no one else to convince of our love.

'But you two must marry. Must, must, must,' Shazia-dadi grumbled every night as we disappeared behind the curtain into our windowless half of the shack.

'Why, dadi? We're not doing anything indecent,' Suleiman would titter, as he lowered my shalwar and his pyjamas. In the ensuing silence, all three of us would fake coughs and sneezes to drown out any chance sounds.

Every hot afternoon, or whenever lines for the two toilets were too long for comfort, Shazia-dadi begged us to leave Mumbai for Namnagar. But Suleiman wanted to be a city tailor for fashionable madams. Besides, where we lived wasn't bad. Ours was the best slum refined refugees could find.

'Imagine,' Suleiman had told me when we were still in Barauli, planning our exit before the Mahant returned to rob and maim us, 'imagine you and me in the heart of Mumbai on the seventeenth floor. What a view! Oh, the breeze! Ah, the silence!'

'What rot!' I'd said. 'You went to Mumbai to look for shelter or take drugs?'

'No, no, Nilofer, really! I saw it today! A slum on the top of a building. It has nine shacks and two toilets with running water.'

Suleiman and my embroiderer uncle rented two adjacent hovels; over a few days they shifted our things from Barauli before bringing us women to this Muslim slum on the terrace of a Muslim skyscraper in a Muslim area. 'The best of the best of the best.' It really is. Although the view still makes me dizzy. And the breeze threatens to take you with it. And climbing seventeen floors (since us slum-dwellers may not use the lifts) can make you utter words you didn't even know you knew.

But did Shazia-dadi have a single good word for the constant breeze or for our company? Hunh! All day she moped or studied the skyline, cursing herself for having begged to come to this hellhole in the sky.

My baby gave her a reason to leave. I vomited every morning for three weeks, taking this syrup and that pill, not realizing all along that I was pregnant.

'But you're not married even!' Shazia-dadi exclaimed on hearing the good news. She pounced on her bags and started packing.

'Don't go, dadi, you'll be all alone in Namnagar,' I said, genuinely concerned.

Shazia-dadi thought I was taunting her and left anyway.

At least Suleiman was ecstatic on hearing about the baby. He had started getting stitching jobs from a local tailor.

One rainy night, while our tin roof was shuddering in the wind and the rain was seeping in upwards from under the door, Suleiman and I began making plans for our coming child. After discussing names and deciding on what kind of sweets to distribute after the birth, the talk got down to money. He put up a brave front, telling me not to worry, he would handle all the expenses. But as every woman knows—or should know—any time a man acts like a man is the time he feels least like one.

My man needed me to step in. And I had to do it without offending him.

'What? What do you mean you are bored?'

'I'm going out of my mind, Suleiman!' I said, the next evening. 'In the village I used to be busy all day: milking the cows, sweeping the house, roaming the fields. Up here...I'm dying up here!'

'So, what do you want to do? You want to roam the city? You want to go out? How are you going to climb seventeen floors up and down every day in your state?'

'I won't. I'll just climb two-three floors.'

'What? What do you mean?'

'Please, Sallu?' I said. 'Please, don't say no, let me work in someone's house below. Please?'

What tantrums men throw! Suleiman's lasted for two days. Two days of shouting and yelling. *Are we servants? Am I so poor? Am I not feeding you?* This. That.

As every woman knows—one ear in, another ear out.

Besides, I wasn't going to be some dirty, ill-mannered servant. I just wanted to be a self-respecting woman doing her job! How could anyone living below refuse to assist a pregnant refugee from their own umaah?

So, the following Sunday morning, while Suleiman was still sleeping, I bathed, put on my finest shalwar-kurta and smudged my eyes with kajal more liberally than usual.

'Where are you going?' Suleiman looked up groggily from his pillow.

I smiled. I bent down to kiss his cheek, and whispered, 'One more word from you and I'll move out this very second.'

Suleiman kissed me back and wished me best of luck.

Numerous are the advantages of living in.

Then I climbed down three storeys to the fourteenth floor and stood in its lobby, wondering which of the four doorbells to ring and ask for work. 1404 or 1401? 1402 or 1403?

Why think so much, I thought. Must be a reason why the first is always the first. Best to start from the first only.

Bismillah.

Flat 1401

'A servant? Mad or what! We have nine daughters. The last thing we need is a servant.'

Flat 1402

(Still in bed, will not rise for another hour no matter who's at the door, it being Sunday morning, a day for waking late, although neither has slept all night, anxious as both are over unpaid credit card bills for the garments, gizmos, gifts and gourmet meals recklessly consumed in conformity with current social aesthetics, and that's how everything happens here, in Flat 1402, slaves to the bandwagon decree, who will not, will *not* rise for another hour no matter *who's* at the door, it being Sunday morning—a day, for waking, late.)

Flat 1403

An hour. Or maybe longer. Doesn't matter. When one is trying to shit, time is unimportant.

So I have been straining on the commode for what seems like an hour, when I notice a drop of blood on my shirt, just below the left pocket. I squint. I wonder if I am seeing things. Could I have strained too hard and burst a vein? I rub my eyes.

When my vision clears, the bloodstain is still there.

I stand up and pull up my trousers. (There is nothing to wash away or flush down. Just like every other 'morning after'. After a successful hit, I need to strain for at least a week before my insides agree to release their waste. By then, the glands on the side of my neck harden and I start smelling of faeces.)

I look into the mirror above the basin. No other stains. My grey shirt is spotless except for this single drop of blood that seems to have travelled almost thirty feet and landed on me so neatly. Strange, right? It was so dark last night; I must have struck that hotelier's artery.

I lick my fingertip and press it to the stain on my shirt. The blood liquefies and it seems, all at once, as if I have touched a fresh wound. Wow. It has been years since I've had blood on my hands. I use a gun now. Earlier, when I used knives or choppers, it used to be a bloodbath in the true sense. I would carry a change of clothes and slip into them in the getaway car.

The bloodstained garments were not to be tossed away; they were to be given to Maamu, our gang-guru; he would cremate the clothes in the balcony of our headquarters.

Like someone accusing himself, I point my blood-specked fingertip at my face. I had forgotten the luscious gloss of blood. I had forgotten its stench of rust—yes, I can smell it now, holding my fingertip near my nostrils, I can smell that faint but unmissable odour of corrosion. I open my mouth. I lick my lips. Should I do it? I have never done it: never tasted blood. Mine, several times; but never the blood of a person I have killed. If I lick this fingertip what would... *did the doorbell just ring*? I prick my ears like a jackal. Like a bhediya. That's what the newspapers call me: Salim Landya, aka Sewri Ka Bhediya.

Ting-nong.

The doorbell rings again. Bhengcho! This doorbell is not supposed to ring! My fingertip grazes my nostrils. Breathing copious amounts of sickening rust-flavoured air, I run out of the bathroom. I grab my gun from the floor. What is this? What is this supposed to mean? Maamu said this flat was vacant! Why would anyone call on a vacant flat!

Holding my loaded gun up, I crouch against the wall, beside the door. 'Who is it?' I ask.

'Salaam-aaley-kum, brother. M-my name is Nilofer,' some woman stammers in a girl-child's voice.

'What do you want?' I ask.

'Work!' she blurts.

Just what I thought. I release the safety latch. 'Then don't waste time,' I shout. 'Let's get this over with!'

'You can open the door, please?' she says.

The patronizing saali. 'Sure,' I say, 'I'll open the door and give you tea-biscuit also. First tell me, madam, how you knew I was here? Who sent you?'

'I–I just rang the bell. I–I did not know who would be there!' she replies.

Liar, I want to shout, *lying madakcho saali*!

I stand up and place my trembling hand on the latch. 'Just wait, haanh,' I say, 'I am opening.'

'Okay, b-brother,' she says, 'I am waiting.'

1…2…3…4…I start counting.

At 20 I will throw open the door and shoot that haraamzaadi's brains out.

Meanwhile, on the Floor Above

Kishore Malhotra rings the bell of flat 1503. A man in a nightsuit answers the door.

'Someday you will catch a horrible disease, linger, and die,' Kishore says and tightens his face. If he was going to be slapped, it would be now. Ten o' clock on a Sunday morning was no time for dismal truths.

'I would hope so,' the resident of 1503 chuckles. Kishore opens his eyes warily. 'Who wants to live for ever? Not me,' the man adds. He crosses his arms and grins at Kishore with absolute serenity.

Kishore is stumped. He only expects the brute in people. What kind of person is this? Through his confusion, Kishore mumbles, 'So how will you pay the high hospital bills? What will happen to your wife and children after you die?'

The resident of 1503 retorts, 'I don't believe in hospitalization, or in children. And I plan to marry money. Anything else?'

Kishore's shirt turns wet with sweat. He is ill-equipped for clever debate; he only means to trigger monetary and biological anxiety, the solution to which is right here, in his folder. He asks this freak one last question, 'But what if your wife also falls ill and both of you are in hospital and all the money runs out?'

The resident rests against his door and frowns. 'Cheer up, boss. What are you? Buddhist?'

No, mister smart aleck, Kishore muses regretfully, and turns to go. *I wish I was, though. I would retreat to the mountains, where the food is free and the air is cool. I am, in fact, an insurance agent and I haven't sold a single policy since I began making the rounds weeks ago. I've tried the slick talk and the smooth moves. I've practised Seven Steps to Successful Sales and improvised eight of my own. People say what I sell is superfluous. Shoo, they say, don't corrupt us with this American mania for surety. Most days I feel like a victim. But of what? I'm not smart enough to fathom.*

'Hello, brother, you didn't say what you were selling!' the man in 1503 jeers. But by then Kishore is on his way down to the fourteenth floor to peddle a policy to flat 1404.

1602, 1503, 1404…the sum of all he does is a deliberate, auspicious nine.

Meanwhile, on the Floor Below

Vinti Kambole puts down her bag of merchandise and rings the bell of flat 1302. A youth in vest and shorts answers the door.

'Is there a lady in the house?' Vinti inquires.

The youth fiddles with the amulet around his neck. 'What you selling?' he asks, when he notices the bag by Vinti's feet.

Her ears redden. 'Ladies' products,' she replies.

The youth smirks, 'What ladies' products?'

Vinti sucks air through her teeth. 'Is there or is there not a lady in the house?'

The youth turns to address someone inside the flat. 'Hey, do we need ladies' products?'

Another youth in a vest and lungi appears. His neck is strung with several amulets. 'What ladies' products?' the second youth asks, a giggle lurking in his voice.

Vinti picks up her bag and turns to go.

'Oh, madam, at least give us a demo!' one of the youths jeers and both break into howls of lynch-mob laughter.

Soon, soon, Vinti calms herself with an assurance, *we'll send you people packing to Pakistan.*

The two voice further indelicacies. But, by then, Vinti is on her way up to the fourteenth floor to sell her goods to flat 1401.

1203, 1302, 1401…the sum of all *she* does is a deliberate, astrologer-approved six.

Moin Chariya

On my way up to the sixteenth floor of Ismat Towers, the lift mysteriously halts on the fourteenth. The metal doors rumble open to reveal a veritable mob in the lobby. My mentor Gaffur Chishti used to say: *Moin, where there people, there always something bad waiting to happen.* So I jump out the lift to investigate.

'Who are you?' I ask the woman outside flat 1403.

'I'm Nilofer,' she bows and says, 'bless me, please, I'm waiting to get work.' I tap her head thrice with my peacock-feather broom.

'And you?' I ask the woman outside flat 1401.

She puts her bag down and joins her hands. 'Myself Vinti, sales girl.' I tap her head too.

I look at the man outside flat 1404. 'What?' he asks.

'What "what"?' I snap back. 'Who are you?'

'I myself am Kishore, sales executive,' he mumbles. I raise my broom. Kishore ignores the cue. 'And who are you?' he asks defiantly.

I look down at myself. Is he blind? Who else dons a black gown and green headscarf, strings beads around his neck and grows a beard for years?

'I don't believe in any baba-vaba,' Kishore says.

'Grrmph!' I jiggle my cloth bag.

Vinti's door—1401—is answered by a hassled-looking matron.

The two start negotiating in whispers. I start the wowgoodgreat chant. The two strike some deal. I intone faster and faster, forgetting words and rehashing new ones into a tremendous stew of goodwill. The back-and-forth ends; Vinti hands over her bag; the matriarch pays her a wad of notes and shuts the door. Vinti turns to us. And?

'I hit the jackpot!' she shrieks. 'The woman has nine grown daughters!'

Wowgoodgreat never fails!

I raise my broom; a solemn Vinti bows to be tapped again and drops ten bucks in my bag.

Kishore blinks at us. 'How did you…' he starts, but quickly turns around—a handicapped man has answered door 1404.

What you sold, I mime at Vinti. She blushes. *You won't understand, baba*, she mimes back.

Just then, the resident of 1404 erupts, 'What a choot!' He jabs a crutch at Kishore, who jumps back in time. 'Telling me I'm going to catch a horrible disease! What do you think polio is? Some time-pass cramp in the legs?' The handicapped man slams the door in Kishore's face.

Hmm. Beautifully vindicated. I stick the broom in my bag and amble to the stairs.

Nilofer comes running. She begs me to stay and bless her. I agree. The other two decide to wait too.

The four of us stand outside flat 1403 for a long, long time. I start with wowgoodgreat and end up with openthebastarddoor!

Five more minutes, still nothing.

'Is anyone even in there?' I grumble, and smack the door with my broom.

'There is, baba!' Nilofer cries. 'Some man spoke to me! He knows I'm waiting for work!'

'Then why he doesn't open?' Vinti asks. Nilofer shrugs.

I lean forward and press my ear to door 1403. I hear: '1, 2, 3, 4, 5, 6, 7, 7, 7, shyaa, saalaa bhengcho…1, 2, 3, 4, 5, 6, 7, 7, 7, abbey kya yaar, saalaa, shyaa…'

'Sst-sst,' I flick a finger at Kishore, 'come, listen.'

He steps forward. 'Some man…' Kishore reports, 'he's counting numbers.' Kishore listens some more, and titters, 'The man counts fine till seven. But then he stumbles, gives filthy curses and starts over, over and over.'

'But why! Why won't he open the door?' Nilofer cries to me.

All three, even baba-doubting Kishore, shrink in automatic obeisance and beseech me with their eyes: *Tell us, baba, why won't the man in 1403 stop counting and open the door?* This morning, on my way here, someone at the bus stop asked: *Do you foresee a number 71 soon?* Last week at a graveyard: *Baba, where is all this going?* Arrey, how am I supposed to know? What must I say to all these people? That I'm clueless? That their guess is better than mine? Can I say such things in these clothes, with the beads around my neck and matted locks on my head?

Everyone has words he isn't allowed to speak, statements and defeats he just can't admit; break out of your role, speak out of character, and the world despises you and discards you.

But then, not everyone craves to be cherished by the world.

Least of all Moin Chariya.

'How am I supposed to know why he won't open? Probably an illiterate who doesn't know to count,' I remark blandly to the three waiting with me outside flat 1403. 'I suggest you all go now, unless you want to wait here for ever.'

That's it.

I start for the stairs.

Midway between the fourteenth and fifteenth, on my way up to the sixteenth floor where a couple has called me to exorcise their Nepali ayah, I hear Vinti remark, 'Let's go, let's go. No use waiting.'

'Hmm,' Nilofer sighs, 'maybe I'll try some other floor.'

'Ha,' Kishore says, 'I knew that fellow was a phoney.'

The two women giggle.

And I?

I pat my proverbial shoulder for having earned, not loose change or cheap devotion, but the seal of disapproval genuine rebels die for.

Flat 1404: Munaf, the Unsuitable Boy

After slamming the door on that choot's face, I just stand near the entrance, hunched over my crutches. I am too exhausted for the walk back to the bedroom.

Two hours later, when my parents return from shopping, I am still standing here.

'Why you got up?' mom cries.

'Someone was at the door,' I say.

'So what!' mom replies, 'Allah, what to do with this boy!'

I am not supposed to answer the door. My parents tell me—and have been telling me for years—to ignore such things. Let the phone keep ringing, they say, let the doorbell chime and the cooker whistle, you please stay where you are. Getting up on my own puts great strain on my torso. The doctor fears I might develop multiple hernias. But if I don't get up, if I remain in my room while things keep ringing-chiming-whistling somewhere in the flat, I become restless, till I can stand it no more, and then I want to torture my spindly legs for being my spindly legs.

Dad puts down several plastic bags on the floor. 'Who was it, Munaf?' he asks.

I raise my head to tell my father how I had come scrambling from the bedroom to answer the door only to be told by some crazed salesman-sort that I was going to catch a horrible disease, linger and die.

But the sight of my father's grey, unshorn face silences me.

'Who was at the door, Munaf?' dad asks again.

'I'm sure it was no one. He gets up just to disobey us,' mom says. She comes and stands behind me. Dad yanks away my crutches. As I start to fall, mom grabs my shoulders, dad lifts my legs, and they carry me to the bedroom and sit me down on the computer chair.

'Now, please stay in your room,' mom says. 'You know who's coming this evening and I have lots of preparations to do. Work on the computer.'

'You know I don't work on Sunday.'

Mom slaps her forehead. 'Then do what you want. But stay here!'

She rests my crutches against the opposite wall, leaving me choice-less.

I remove a photo from my shirt-pocket. The girl in the photo is coming this evening. Her name is Sophiya. She and her parents are coming to see me. They called this morning before boarding the bus in Ahmednagar. They know I have polio; I suppose it was the first thing the matchmaker told Sophiya's parents about me, followed by an in-depth account of my father's immense wealth. If today, after meeting with me, Sophiya feels she can tolerate my crutches and the braces on my legs, our families will go ahead with our marriage.

Did I say 'marriage'? More like the shifting of a burden.

In the photo—which arrived via a circuitous route involving several strangers and relatives—Sophiya is in a red shalwar-kurta with red lipstick and red cheeks. She is holding a red rose and is standing against an immense poster showing a field full of deep-red roses. Everything else about Sophiya is either powder white or jet black.

'I think she's lovely,' mom had said. Dad had studied the photo and agreed guardedly. 'You have no reason to complain,' mom told me.

Not 'reason'. Mom meant 'right'. I have no right to complain.

Sophiya isn't the first girl. I have rejected all the substandard out-of-towners the matchmaker has been sending my way for the last three years. Sophiya seems no better or worse than the earlier eight, but this time I won't refuse. I am twenty-five now, and after fifteen years of attending to me full-time, of fetching my crutches and postponing their vacations, I believe it's only fair that my parents be relieved.

Evening comes.

Sophiya and her parents arrive.

Sitting in a row on our sofa, all three look frayed and dusty after the nine-hour bus journey. It doesn't surprise me that Sophiya is nothing like her photo. I am neither disappointed by her modest bust nor let down by her dusky complexion. Just a mild pang of panic when I imagine having to wake up beside one woman—just this one—for the rest of my life.

'Money-wise everything is...?' Sophiya's father asks.

Dad nods. 'Munaf has his own e-business, you know, of selling books on the internet. Besides, everything I own is his.'

Sophiya's mother inquires about the extent of my handicap.

'Oh, it's nothing much,' mom says. 'Would you like to see Munaf walk around?'

Sophiya's parents say 'yes'. They have been staring unabashedly at my special shoes. Their daughter is sitting between them, looking down at her plate heaped with the snacks mom has prepared.

Mom brings my crutches and rests one on either side of my armchair. I look at her, but her eyes are expressionless. I look at dad. He is staring at the floor. They always do this: they always make me parade my handicap. And I always refuse.

Seeing me linger, Sophiya's father feels forced to say, 'It's okay, beta, doesn't matter, forget it.'

'No,' I say, 'you should know what you're getting into.'

I sit up. I straighten my leg-braces. Then I dig my palms into the armrests to lift my torso off the chair, when an urgent command shoots across the room: 'Don't! Please!'

I look up in shock. Sophiya is looking at me. It's the first thing she has said since arriving.

Suddenly everything seems awry—it is as if a spinner has delivered a fast ball, as if Kenya has won the World Cup. That voice doesn't belong to the garish out-of-town girl in the photo; it is not the voice of the skinny thing sitting between her parents on our sofa. The voice, that request, and the immense benevolence in those words belong to a woman, not some girl but a woman who, with just two words, has rendered my parents unnecessary.

I sit back with relief, the kind I haven't known in years. I mumble 'thank you'. Sophiya nods and lowers her gaze.

Ten minutes later all three troop out, with Sophiya's parents promising to notify us of their decision in a few days. But it doesn't matter any more. Even before she has left our flat I have sworn to myself: if Sophiya says no, I will remain a bachelor for ever.

'Please, God, please let them not say no,' mom grumbles while clearing the coffee table.

Yes, God, I look at the ceiling dreamily, *please*, *yes*.

A Digression With a Purpose

Now all Hamida wanted was to be Rafiq's fourth wife.

She had, of course, planned on being his first. But, during summer, when Hamida returned to Ahmednagar after a week at her uncle's home in Jalgaon, she found that Rafiq had married his aunt's daughter.

They met a day later at their secret spot in the park. Rafiq fell at Hamida's feet and swore he couldn't help getting married, his father had forced him, and he had had no opportunity to mention his prior—albeit unofficial and unknown—commitment to Hamida. Hamida shrugged sportingly. They kissed for seven minutes. Later, when they stood hugging against an abandoned tonga, Hamida said, 'Tell your father about us, Rafiq. I don't mind, I can be your second wife, but tell him you want to marry me.'

'Okay,' Rafiq said, and they kissed till it became dark.

Several weeks later, Rafiq went to Delhi to collect payments for his father's business. He was supposed to return in a week. He took three. And when he came back to Ahmednagar, it was with his second wife—another cousin—this time his mother's brother's daughter. Hamida insisted on a meeting the same evening. An anxious and harried Rafiq arrived an hour late. 'Circumstances were such that...'

'What? What were the circumstances?' Hamida demanded to know.

'They caught me kissing her and forced me to marry her.'

'Oh, I wish I too was your cousin,' Hamida said wistfully. 'Tell your father about us, Rafiq. I don't mind, I can be your third wife even, but at least now tell your father to marry us.'

'I will, I will,' Rafiq said, but he didn't have time to kiss; he had to hurry home to pacify his first wife.

Two months later, when Rafiq came and said, 'Bad news,' Hamida didn't even flinch. It was her twenty-first birthday; she had brought a piece of chocolate halwa for Rafiq. Hamida dropped the sweet and squatted on the ground as Rafiq said he didn't want to, *he didn't*, but was being forced to marry his sister-in-law's sister whose parents had been killed in a riot.

'You have turned my life into a shoddy joke,' Hamida whispered.

Rafiq didn't hear her, though, and continued, 'Number one took it quite well this time; but I think number two is waiting to throw a tantrum at some choice moment. Wives, I tell you!'

Now all Hamida wanted was to be Rafiq's fourth wife. There was, however, a problem: Rafiq couldn't afford a fourth wife. Not unless she came with money enough for herself and at least two others. 'My parents are paupers!' Hamida cried. But Rafiq, who had started to look a decade older than his age of twenty-four, said there was nothing he could do. Much as he wanted to marry Hamida, money, and the shortage thereof, was too malignant a reality to be obscured by love.

Now all Hamida wanted was money. Short of working hard and prostitution, she thought of all the ways that could bring her immediate and immense wealth. She recalled that her friend, Sophiya, who lived behind the bakery, had been to Mumbai a few days ago to see a rich boy.

Hamida rushed to Sophiya's house. She called Sophiya out and asked, 'Listen, you are marrying that boy from Mumbai or no?'

'I've not decided as yet,' Sophiya said.

'Okay, but decide quickly. If you are not interested, better give me the matchmaker's number.'

Sophiya was amazed. 'But, Hamida, that boy is handicapped. You yourself said you'd rather remain a spinster than marry someone with polio.'

'I know, I know, but...' Hamida told her friend her entire story.

By the time Hamida was finished, Sophiya was ready to vomit. 'So, basically, after I divorce that cripple, I will take his money and come back and marry Rafiq. Good, no?' Hamida beamed at her own cleverness.

It was at that moment, paralysed by her friend's grin, that Sophiya decided—enough, no more dithering, she would marry Munaf, the polio-ridden boy from Mumbai. If for no other reason than to save him from women like Hamida.

And to protect herself from men like Rafiq.

Jeyna-bi, the Buffet Fiend

Their wedding was a stupendous success!

Munaf's parents had spent so much money decorating the marriage hall and there was such a variety of things to eat, that everybody was asking, 'Who's the caterer? Who's the caterer?' (No, not me. The caterer was Lucky Hotel.) Then everybody asked, 'Who's the decorator? Who's the decorator?' (Again, not me.) And *then* I heard two women gossiping, and one of them asked, 'By the way, who's the matchmaker?'

Who else? Me! Jeyna-bi!

I was hard to miss in my fluorescent orange burkha.

When I went up on stage to wish the wedded pair, Munaf's father widened his eyes and remarked, 'Jeyna-bi, wherever I look I am only seeing you this evening. What's the plan, haanh?'

'Allaaaah!' I squealed, and buried my face in his wife's arm. Munaf's father is such a naughty boy, I tell you!

As I was descending the stage, two women and a man were awaiting me at the bottom of the steps. I stopped and inhaled deeply before plunging headlong into all those people clamouring for Jeyna-bi, Jeyna-bi, Jeyna-bi. They formed a line behind me. Our procession marched towards the buffet section. One by one parents would come up, shove their marriageable child in my face, and tell me everything about him or her since birth.

At one point the father of a divorced optician said, 'Jeyna-bi, just look behind you!'

What? There was nothing.

'Don't you see?' the man cried. 'Your line is longer than the line at the stage!'

I strained my eyes. No, it wasn't. There was no one behind me.

'You've grown old, Jeyna-bi, get your eyes checked. I'm telling you, your line is longer,' the optician's father gushed as he steered his son in my path. 'Meet my Tahir. Just look at him and tell me honestly: can you make out he's divorced?'

I wiped my tears. My line longer than the stage line? Allah-be-thanked! It may have been Munaf and Sophiya's wedding but this was turning out to be one of the grandest nights of my life!

I became overexcited as usual. When I reached the buffet table, I got carried away like always and had two-two three-three helpings of all the dishes on offer.

Really, at weddings I need someone to accompany me. I need someone to dig their nails into my arm and hiss, *Go slow on the free food, understand?*

So I ate and ate and ate, because there was no one to tell me to stop.

Halfway through dessert, I felt a spicy burp rearing its head. I pushed back my chair. 'Oohh maa...' I groaned. I loosened my shalwar. I began contorting my torso—front to back, left to right. Other guests saw me thrashing about and came forward to help. I motioned everybody to step back, give me space, I was only trying to burp! But one idiot woman panicked—she removed her leather chappal and pressed it on my face. She thought I was having a fit!

That was it.

'Jeyna-bi vomited! Jeyna-bi vomited!'

'Big deal. She always does.'

Tch, I don't know how it happened. They had to carry me to the bathroom. The stuff was all over my burkha. Swear-to-Allah, I try my best to control. But every time I just…I go nuts.

On returning from the bathroom, I pulled my veil down like the shutter of a shop and hid in a corner for the rest of the evening.

'Jeyna-bi?' a woman tried to raise my veil.

There was only one woman who would dare to lift Jeyna-bi's veil. One very obnoxious woman. 'Go away, Yasmin-bai,' I said.

She squatted between my legs and peered up my veil. 'I heard you vomited? Feeling better now?'

I shut my veil tight. 'Go away, I don't want to talk to anyone.'

'Ya Ali!' Yasmin-bai said. 'See no, just like a child!' She sat down beside me. Then she started her usual nonsense: 'Seen someone for my Nawaz?'

Allah! First that optician's father flattering me with lies, then that puke bath, and now this idiot lady droning in my ear: 'I beg you, Jeyna-bi, find a girl for my son. Please, Jeyna-bi, I am only asking for a simple girl, not some princess, just someone who knows how to handle money. I will feed her good-good things…'

'SHUT UP!' I flung back my veil.

Yasmin-bai clutched her chest.

'Are you *retarded*?' I screamed. 'Where will the couple sleep in your one-room flat? Under the *bed*?'

Yasmin-bai looked down like an admonished girl.

I went for the jugular. 'Don't think I don't know! I keep an eye on everyone. Your Nawaz is a number one bum. Doesn't do any work, doesn't come for any functions. How will he feed his wife? He'll make his wife *work*?'

Yasmin-bai shook her head; she started to say something.

But I was finished with that stupid wedding, and I was finished with Yasmin-bai.

'Forgive me.' I stood up. 'I may be a gluttonous matchmaker, but I don't deliberately shove girls in the fire! Before opening your mouth so wide you should have at least checked to see if you have the teeth! Khuda-haafiz!'

Yasmin-bai, Nawaz's Mother

But my Nawaz has started working! Instead of taunting me and *my* big mouth, if that Jeyna-bi had kept hers shut, I would have told her that my son has finally started working! Yes, okay, I know, like all young men even my Nawaz went through a little idle patch.

But then, last week, he returned home one afternoon and announced, 'Ammi, I've found work.' (The three sweetest words a son can tell his widowed mother; and also, *Ammi, I'm getting married.* Soon, soon, I'm sure—as soon as that Jeyna-bi obliges.)

'I'll need abbu's sherwanis,' my son said. 'We still have them, right? Those two black sherwanis abbu wore?'

'What?' I screeched. 'You namakool!' I seized Nawaz by his collar. 'Just get out!' I dragged him to the door. 'You just get out of this house your abbu bought with honest money! In this respectable Medina, I will not allow you to make even one corrupt aana!'

'Ammi, stop it, leave me! Have you gone mad? I just asked for abbu's sherwanis!'

'You think I don't know? Haanh? You think I don't know who wears sherwanis in this day and age? No, Nawaz...' I snapped my fingers. 'Out, just get out! Go be a politician elsewhere!'

'You think I am becoming a politician? Are you mad? Do I look mad to you?'

'You are not becoming a politician?' I let go of my son's collar.

'Of course not, ammi!' Nawaz adjusted his shirt. 'I am not *that* depraved!'

'Haash!' The day suddenly went from morose Moharram to festive Eid. 'God bless you, beta.'

I bent under the bed for the trunk; from it, I fished out the bundled remains of my dead husband's material life and unwrapped the two black coats. Nawaz grabbed one and put it against his body, craning his neck out to see. 'Damn, too long, looks more like a dress than a sherwani.'

Pretending like I couldn't care less, I asked, 'So what you going to do wearing this fancy dress? What job you got, haanh?'

'You won't understand,' Nawaz said. 'I'm going to try this on.' He barged off to the balcony. In this one-room-per-flat colony, everybody changes in their balcony. We bare ourselves to the outside world so the ones who matter inside won't see us exposed.

When Nawaz returned, I could see the sherwani was loose— too long and roomy. He doesn't have the appetite or vigour of his father who lived big, spoke loudly and walked with long strides. As if to compensate for his dead father's excesses, Nawaz moves around suspiciously, eats like a miser and speaks in measured tones.

'Don't alter them, please, this is all I have of your father,' I begged, when Nawaz said he would put the precious garments under the local tailor's scissors.

He looked at me like I was his biggest enemy, 'You're right, ammi. I mustn't alter these sherwanis. I *want* to look like a joker.'

I smiled, perplexed by the disgust on my son's face.

That was that. From that day on, Nawaz dresses up in his father's finery every morning: the unaltered sherwani, the bunching pyjamas and a dark-brown embroidered skullcap. Then he gathers a pile of faded books and leaves.

If only I knew how to read, or if I had a daughter-in-law whom I could conspire with, I would know what my Nawaz was up to.

Badru, Nawaz's Paanwallah

One day I will turn red.

Not like Bengal.

Literally!

One day the red tinge of kattha will spread from my fingernails to my palms, arms, neck, chest, legs, penis, toes. Everything will be a healthy bloody red. Serves me right for selling paan. Such an addictive thing. It is as if the colony's women specifically give birth to sons so that when they grow up they can hang around my booth all day like weaklings craving daily—sometimes hourly—fixes of my green, aromatic, enfolded bundles of bliss. And I always pack a sucker punch. Whether they like it or not, I finger a solid coating of white lime on the betel leaf to make my customers' tongues burn and their brains buzz. With a thrill like that for just two bucks, who wouldn't want more and more every boring day?

Men form cheap habits so they can be happy quickly, any time, anywhere. Women, they want jewellery and a nice house and expensive visits to their parents' homes—nothing your local tobacconist can deliver. So women remain sad, and are further angered by the easy happiness their menfolk have perpetual access to.

But I am not without scruples. If you are a youth from a good family, I will sell you nothing. You can walk a kilometre to some other immoral paanwallah for all I care and stuff your body with useless flavours. What I sell is injurious to health. I will have no share in destroying someone if he isn't already flawed. Like that boy from B3-2 building. Nawaz. Seen him growing up, I have. Since last week he has started packing two sweet paans every morning.

'You want to be a politician or something?' I had asked Nawaz, 'What's with the sherwani and skullcap?' He didn't answer, just stood quietly waiting for the paans.

On the first day I refused to sell him any. 'Son,' I said to Nawaz, 'I can do without your business. The people I sell this stuff to deserve it. They are rotten. But not you. Better stay away from all this paan-vaan.' But Nawaz would have none of it, and threatened to buy the paans elsewhere.

I may be scrupulous, but I too have to survive, don't I!

'More kattha, Badru!' Nawaz said. 'Lot's more kattha. I want my mouth to be red like a pomegranate.'

I dipped my fingers in the brick-brown mixture and lobbed some more on the betel leaf.

'More kattha, Badru! More kattha!' Nawaz spurred me.

'You gone bonkers or what?' I said. 'More than this and your mouth will dry up forever like a eunuch's privates. This kattha is potent stuff, you know,' I counselled like a sage and packed the paans into separate packets.

Now, every morning, Nawaz pockets the two paans, piles his books on his cycle's carrier seat and rides off looking like the destitute prince of some newly impoverished territory.

Abhay, Nawaz's Student

Ah, there's Nawaz-saab riding into our lane. On entering our gate, he will slide off his cycle, chain it to a railing in the car park and climb up to our flat. For the two hours he teaches me Urdu poetry, maroon liquid will repeatedly streak down the sides of his mouth. He will wipe it away with a stained handkerchief and continue to expound.

Yesterday, Nawaz-saab asked me to memorize this verse:

Ashkon samad sa kufiya ul aasoon
Maghreeb naahid-azaan ulfati nastaeen

Ah, these words, these words! What rhythm! What magnificence! It is a couplet by Faiz. One of his very first verses. Nawaz-saab says, when Faiz first recited these words at a gathering of fellow poets, an eavesdropping businessman swooned at their sheer beauty. Today, Nawaz-saab will reveal the couplet's meaning.

'You must first get accustomed to the sound, Abhay,' he says. 'Urdu poetry is to be secreted like silk. Savour every strand, Abhay, savour every strand.'

Nawaz-saab is right. When basking in the sun of Urdu poetry, there's no use hurrying; I must let its beauty and wisdom invade me like a tan.

I don't know Urdu. I don't know Urdu and I will never

forgive my parents for it. Will never forgive them for such a dry, artless upbringing, devoid of culture or beauty—no music, no ideas, nothing. Money—that's the be-all and end-all of the artistry my lineage has ever dabbled in.

I tried explaining this to Swati. She would have none of it. 'I'm sorry, Abhay, you're just too crude! We have tremendous physical chemistry, agreed, but we can't be in bed all the time. What about the mornings or during meals? What do we talk of then? How many *pro*grammes you *de*bugged? I want someone immersed in life, someone who can buy me diamonds while fascinating me with his take on Pynchon's works.'

I heaved tragically, 'Okay, Swati, okay. I may not have read Pynchon, but I'll show you. When I return from India, you'll see. I'll be arty, just as you like. Please, will you marry me then?'

She tightened her grip on my hair. 'God, Abhay, if you don't like all this stuff, it's okay. Maybe I'm just not the one for you.'

'No, Swati, no!' I looked up from between her thighs. 'You're the one for me! Give me two months. When I come back to Boston, I promise I'll be dripping with the humanities like you won't believe.'

Swati yielded and I flew to India two days later for a vacation with a mission: the artification of Abhay Joshi.

Mom and dad were confounded by my outbursts. 'The woman I love won't marry me because I'm a ruffian! You know how that feels, dad? DD, Hindi films, Hindi songs—that's all you both ever gave me. I'm going to lose the woman I love because you two couldn't care about life's finer things!'

As I recovered from jetlag, my befuddled begetters frantically arranged to pack in a childhood's worth of refinement in two months. Dad visited a sitarist in Bhandup to request a crash course in the instrument. 'How crashed a course did you have in mind?' the sitarist asked. 'A month and a half long,' dad replied. The man doubled over hysterically.

After spreading the word around, mom remained luckless. She gifted me something by Narayan and took to masterminding daily feasts.

'This place is supposed to be a motherlode of culture!' I exclaimed one night over dinner. 'Where's the goddamn culture? I don't see any culture. Where's the culture?'

Days passed. Narayan became progressively unchallenging, and my chances with Swati lessened by the minute. 'Maybe some other girl…?' mom suggested and fled to escape my cold stare.

Then a call came, in the third week, for dad. It was Firoz-saab, the sitar instructor who had laughed him out. He was sorry, and wanted to help. Dad put his hand over the phone and mimed across the room: *Would I be interested in learning Urdu poetry? Ghalib, Faiz, Sheikh?*

Would I ever!

'Expect Nawaz-saab tomorrow morning,' Firoz-saab said, 'and please don't offend him by haggling. For the revelation of a precious and life-altering body of Urdu poetry, three thousand rupees is surely a joke.'

For a life with Swati, sixty dollars were truly nothing.

When mom opened the door the next morning at ten, it was as if our epiphanies had come alive. She bowed while moving aside to let Nawaz-saab in.

'Please,' dad invited him in, 'come. Have a seat.'

The sherwani-clad man with fine features and a mouth red

with paan looked around with the creative nervousness of an artist. On his way to the sofa, he banged his toes against a leg of the dining chair and nearly tripped over an edge of the carpet. Then he dropped the pile of books he was carrying. Dad helped him gather them. When Nawaz-saab finally managed to sit down, I believe all three of us considered it a personal accomplishment.

Mr Joshi, Nawaz's Student's Father

He sat across us, staring like a Buddha at the floor near his feet. Nawaz-saab seemed just slightly older than Abhay. Chunky beads of sweat swelled on his forehead and rivulets flowed down his sideburns into his sherwani's collar. Must not have been earning enough to afford square meals—the poor fellow was practically floating in his clothes!

So it was all about this. Abhay sneering at our favourite TV shows and groaning at our nightly radio programmes. Abhay flinging aside our Reader's Digests and Chitralekhas. The past three weeks of making Shilpa and me feel like disastrous parents. This scrawny man with a mouthful of paan was to amend Abhay's dull upbringing by teaching him Urdu poetry.

Abhay says we are cultureless. That his mother and I never exposed him to the arts; never made provision for the refinement that comes from contact with sublimity. Doesn't Abhay realize? He is our art. He is my mural, my novella and the verse I invested my years in. Instead of providing for him, would he rather I had painted and his mother sung?

Intoxicated by the self-obsessed psychological hyperawareness his stay in America has triggered, Abhay thinks he can demand answers and justifications from everyone. I suspect he has the courage to do so only with us, his parents. His girlfriend in America has him whirling on the edge of her whimsical fingernail, customizing Abhay as her fancy dictates. It makes Shilpa angry at times. But I say, 'Let go, let go. In a month Abhay will return to America. Then we can resume our peaceful routine.'

Children overestimate their importance in their parents' lives. Towards Abhay I feel a cool detachment. When he told me how much his American employer pays him, I had felt some astonishment that this youngster, whom the world is wanting to own, is a product of *me*! But otherwise I feel towards him a neutral objectivity. Abhay must never learn of this, of course. He must believe my enthusiasm during his visits to India.

When I married, I fell in love with Shilpa. Two years later, I lost my heart to my daughter Avantika. And three years after that, Abhay became my world. Now? No one. I am in love with no one. I have replaced them all with nothingness. A blank mind. Borrowed opinions. Manufactured entertainment. A thriving gift shop for my livelihood and a hard bed as per my tastes. What else is there to life? Music? Painting? *Poetry*? Bah! Art is for those who are clumsy at real life. Such people squirrel away everything—memories, emotions and opinions—for later. When you love like the ocean and wound like Christ, art and beauty ooze from everything you do.

Abhay needs to become a parent, I think. And so does Swati, his girlfriend. They need to snap out of the clinical preoccupation with the mind and feel the mess, sweat, dirt, blood and mucous of real life. The day Abhay hears the first screech of their newborn, I am certain all this regret over an artless upbringing and head-breaking over Urdu poetry will seem a frivolous waste of time. Children are the ultimate grounding for the rootless.

I just hope Abhay isn't as unfortunate as me, to fall out of love with his own offspring. Or maybe…

Maybe when it does happen—when Abhay's heart doesn't beat for his child any more—this Urdu poetry will stave off the nothingness and give Abhay something to look forward to. Maybe this brief contact with art will be all that remains. Could I also find something to look forward to other than the shop, a cricket match, or the next meal? Is there really a way out of this nothingness? What the hell is Abhay going on about?

Nawaz- 'saab'

So one day even Mr Joshi decided to learn Urdu poetry. He said, 'Nawaz-saab, I want to sample profundity before it is too late. My son says you are an excellent teacher. Let me sit with Abhay, please, you can teach us both.'

I almost swallowed the entire paan in alarm. I asked the old man if he knew Urdu.

'How difficult can it be?' he asked. 'It's mostly like Gujarati, no?'

Abhay widened his eyes in angry disbelief. 'What're you saying, dad? Urdu's nothing like Gujju! All those Persian words and complex sentence structures!'

Mr Joshi grinned. 'Okay, okay, if I don't understand, Nawaz-saab can explain to me. Fine?'

I countered discouragingly: an additional student would mean extra fees.

The old man agreed to pay an equal amount for himself—in advance!

My gloom turned a deeper shade of black.

The next morning Mr Joshi received me, dressed in a starched white kurta-pyjama. He trailed behind me on our way to the balcony. 'Nawaz-saab, I haven't learnt anything new in decades, you know. Since I started the shop, my life has only been about profit and loss and...' he dried up mid-sentence when we entered the sunny balcony where Abhay was sitting cross-legged on a rug. Abhay shifted aside to make room for his father. The old man placed a hand on his son's shoulder and began settling down with dying-animal groans. My ammi does that too.

'Okay, Nawaz-saab,' Mr Joshi said, rubbing his palms like a gurkha on a cold night, 'we are ready for Urdu poetry.'

I sat on a settee facing them and said, 'First, I will explain the verse I asked Abhay to memorize yesterday. Then, I will teach three–four new verses.'

Mr Joshi nodded with wide-eyed absorption, while his son, usually receptive and eager, looked around dazed and sullen. A senior person's over-enthusiasm can be quite irritating. To quell the old man's exuberance, I asked Abhay to recite the verse.

Abhay nodded gravely. He closed his eyes and said, 'Bukhara-e junoon shabo khayalon roo maaheer… Bukhara-e junoon shabo khayalon roo maaheer—Laila ilmata jaan-bajaan sekha.'

The hair on my skin bristled. Abhay had repeated the first two lines like they did in films.

'What was that? Junoon *what* khayalon?' Mr Joshi asked with intense interest.

'Shabo khayalon,' Abhay mumbled.

The old man narrowed his eyes and begged, 'Please, Abhay, say it again na, it was so beautiful!'

Abhay obliged with hesitation.

On hearing it again, Mr Joshi swayed his head as if in a trance, 'Wow, Laila ilmata jaan-bajaan sekha, simply superb! Nawaz-saab, quickly, the meaning!'

I studied the floor around my toes with a poetic pensiveness. *Bukhara-e junoon shabo khayalon roo maaheer—Laila ilmata jaan-*

bajaan sekha. The meaning. My jaw shifted from side to side, pounding the paan in my mouth to oblivion. The meaning. I picked up one of my books, flipped through it and stared at the Arabic squiggles across some random page.

'Er, Nawaz-saab, the meaning?' Mr Joshi coughed politely.

I looked up with a start. 'Ah, yes, the meaning.'

I swallowed a bit of the pungent paan liquid, squeezed the pulp into one cheek, and began, 'Measles…'

I went to the window. I spat a perfect arc of blood-red juice and returned to my seat. 'Measles…'

I looked at their faces. The old man seemed on the verge of an orgasm. Abhay's indifference had vanished too. Both were now looking at me like they were jewellers and I was the penniless customer who had swallowed a precious diamond that they would do anything to get back.

'Measles…that…that cause multicolour mumps to…to…to…'

I crumpled my face. 'I cannot do this!'

I stood up. 'Sorry, the mood is gone. I cannot teach poetry today.'

I shivered my hand over my skull. 'I feel frazzled!'

I stormed out the door, ran down the stairs, and cycled like a maniac all the way home.

A Prelude to the Death of Sohail Tambawala

Standing in the kitchen, waiting for the pressure cooker to whistle, Mrs Joshi absent-mindedly traced the letters a-v-a-n-t-i-k-a on the wall with her wet finger.

Earlier in the morning, while mulling over a crossword clue, she had doodled a-v-a-n-t-i-k-a on the edge of the newspaper; on coming to, she had drawn several lines across what she had scribbled. But the kitchen, unlike the newspaper and the rest of the house, was Mrs Joshi's domain. Reading the watermark on the wall, she experienced a severe shortage of breath, like the absence of a lung named a-v-a-n-t-i-k-a.

The cooker hissed its last. Mrs Joshi heard the main door bang open and someone rushing out. Her husband came to the kitchen. She flung a handful of water on the wall. *I will divorce you if you take her name in this house again*, Mr Joshi had warned his wife, and then he had mouthed a line from one of the c-grade potboilers he loved to watch: *this day forth, that girl is dead for me.*

'What are you up to?' Mr Joshi cried on entering the kitchen. 'Why you throwing water on the wall?'

Mrs Joshi shook her head and continued rolling a chapatti. 'Poetry session over so soon?' she asked.

Mr Joshi poured himself water. 'Yes, Nawaz-saab wasn't up

for teaching today. What to say of these creative types.' He gulped the water noisily and replaced the steel glass on the kitchen stand. 'How much longer for lunch?'

'Soon,' Mrs Joshi said.

'How much longer for lunch?' Abhay came and asked a few minutes later.

'Soon,' Mrs Joshi said.

After lunch, while gargling at the basin, Mr Joshi asked, 'What's for tea?'

From the bedroom, Abhay yelled, 'Mom, make something light for dinner, okay!'

Mrs Joshi was at the table, still ploughing through her meal. After wolfing down their food, father and son thought nothing of getting up, leaving the lady of the house to finish alone like a labourer. Today, she ignored her family's requests, busy as she was with tracing Avantika's telephone number in the gravy on her plate.

Abhay got ready and left. Mr Joshi turned on the TV in the bedroom and immediately began cheering, 'Yeaaa! Tendlya, saala, superb yaar!'

Mrs Joshi licked her fingers clean. Her eyes darted about. It was now or… She picked up the cordless lying on the dining table and dialled Avantika's number. *Divorce me*, she thought, *throw me out, but I will speak to my daughter*.

Mrs Joshi was not supposed to call. 'Don't na, ma, let me live my life,' Avantika had said. And so Avantika called once a month, precisely, on the last day of the month; first, with a warning blank call, and then again, five minutes later, to inform her mother that she was still alive, working hard, eating well, happy with her husband, okay, bye.

Yesterday was the last day of March, but there were no blank calls.

And last night Mrs Joshi dreamt her daughter had died.

She clutched the cordless, awaiting an answer at the other end. Stock apologies welled up in Mrs Joshi's throat to pacify Avantika if she picked up the phone.

Avantika still hadn't forgiven her family for disapproving of the short, swarthy, plain-looking man she had brought home and introduced as her fiancé. *This* was Sohail Tambawala? Yes, this was Avantika's Sohail, a salaried nobody who lived alone in a tiny rented suburban flat. Next to Avantika's overweight frame, he had seemed reedy, like the gist of an actual man. While Abhay struggled to hold back his chuckles and as Mr Joshi rolled his eyes, Avantika had battled hard on behalf of the visitor, repeating aloud the answers he mumbled, serving him snacks he was too shy to take himself. She had protected Sohail like a bodyguard, refusing to leave him alone, shooting down the uncomfortable questions her father had tried to ask: *What does your father do? Are you staunch? Do you eat beef?*

After Sohail left, Mr Joshi snorted, 'Where did you find that sample, Avi?'

He was a friend of a colleague, Avantika replied calmly.

'And you actually intend to marry that sorry thing?'

Yes, she was going to marry that sorry thing.

'Honestly, we don't mind that he's Mohammedan. But we do mind that he has the personality of a peon.'

Fair enough, Avantika said, maybe a peon-type was best suited for a girl everyone called Tuntun, mottee, haathi, jhaadhi, appu, or, if they were feeling less cruel, fat-ass.

'Slim down, then see how many boys I line up for you.'

No, she would not slim down, she could not slim down, she hadn't eaten properly in years and she'd had enough. Regardless of what her family thought, she adored Sohail, but that was beside the point. He adored her, *he adored her*, and Avantika challenged her father to find another man who would feel that way.

'Must be something wrong in his head.'

Avantika married Sohail some weeks later. Mr Joshi had tried to stop his daughter, dressed in her bridal best, from leaving for the court. 'Dad, please, just leave me alone,' she had said. Her father had granted her her wish. Now even her brother, it seemed, had abandoned all memory of Avantika. On his current visit to India, anxious about making himself tolerable to his girlfriend in America, Abhay hadn't once asked after his big sister.

Suddenly, mid-ring, Avantika's phone was answered with a clamour of knocks and bangs. Mrs Joshi thought she heard a struggle for the receiver at Avantika's end. 'Avi… Avi…' she gasped in panic.

In the bedroom, Mr Joshi had muted the TV and leaned back in his chair to see if his wife was done with lunch. He saw her with the cordless. 'Who are you phoning, Shilpa?'

'Hello! Hang on, please!' Avantika cried out in the background.

Mrs Joshi heard scratches and scrapes, as if the telephone wire was being wound around someone's neck.

'Sohail?' Avantika nearly shouted into the receiver. 'Sohail?'

'No, Avi, it's mummy!' Mrs Joshi said. 'What's happening, beta? Avi?'

'Nothing's happening, mom. I just dropped the phone.'

Oh! She had dropped the phone. Mrs Joshi felt her insides lining up in the shape of a smile. Avantika—still the awkward butter-fingered girl she secretly loved more than Abhay.

'What happened, mom? Why have you called?'

Mrs Joshi ignored the snub. 'What else to do. Why you didn't phone me yesterday?'

'Who is it, Shilpa?' Mr Joshi was now at the hall's entrance. 'Who are you speaking to?'

'Ya, I got busy. Listen, mom, I'll call you later, okay…'

Mrs Joshi whispered, 'Avi, wait!' But her husband heard the whispered words and froze at the doorway.

'What, mom. I'm in a hurry.'

Mrs Joshi, scared solid, gaped at her husband's face.

'Mom, speak! I don't have time!'

Mr Joshi gestured his wife to continue. 'Stop acting silly. Go on, talk. I'm not going to kill you.'

With a suspicious eye on her husband, Mrs Joshi stammered, 'Avi, Avi you are happy, no?'

'What?'

'Avi you are happy or no…just tell me if you…'

'God, mom! Ya, I'm very, very happy. Okay? Bye!'

Avantika, the Idealist

I put down the receiver.

I've done all I can. There's no way out. I have to go to the police. If I don't, Sohail's supervisor will. And then there's no telling how the cops will ill-treat me for failing to report that my husband left his office three days ago, on Monday evening, and never came home.

The phone rings again. This time I don't pounce on it like an animal. 'Sohail?'

'No.' It is Mr Das, my husband's supervisor. 'Mrs Avantika, this is the last time I am asking for the password. I need the password to your husband's PC, understand? Otherwise I will have to go and report…'

'Do what you want!' I hang up with such force that the receiver's unbreakable plastic develops a hairline crack.

Mr Das doesn't know. He thinks Sohail is being wilful by not showing up at work. All he needs is the password to Sohail's workstation. If he doesn't get it, he will approach the authorities.

Before he does, I must go to them myself.

What else can I do? I begin pacing our hall. What-else-can-I-do? No matter what, people like us don't go to the police. We suffer, we tolerate, we mediate, we pay antisocial men to settle sticky deadlocks, but we don't go to the police. Not unless we wish to be harassed instead of assisted. My stupid, irresponsible husband has only misplaced himself without a trail. I know of people who have had their kin murdered and they've not even lodged a missing-person complaint.

That bloody password! If it wasn't for the password Mr Das wouldn't even care. Sohail isn't the type one misses. On Tuesday, the first day of Sohail's absence from work, I had made a series of password suggestions: *Tika* (what Sohail calls me), *Fehmida* (his mother's name), *Puzo* (Sohail loves the Godfather). Mr Das tried them all; none worked. And I thought I knew my husband well. 'Where in god's name is Sohail? Just ask him!' Mr Das demanded. I would have waited for ever for Sohail to show up; I would have fabricated an elaborate lie to explain my husband's disappearance—to others and to myself. But Mr Das isn't buying my excuses any more. That bitch of a password! No way out. I have go to the police before Mr Das does.

Sounds at the main door. Someone's fumbling with the lock. Is it…

No, it isn't Sohail. The servant enters the flat with her set of keys. I have been at home for the third day in a row, missing work. As Gangu-bai catwalks past the hall to the kitchen, she looks at me pointedly. Yes, my dear, I know that I am intruding on your private space and time. But this is my flat!

I bathe and put on the shalwar-kameez Sohail's sister sent from Dubai. I never wear it. The material is a clingy nylon. But at least it is a dull orange—the closest colour I have to saffron.

I look in the mirror. No, still too secular. I need more. I need…

'Gangu-bai!'

She comes to the bedroom. 'What?'

'Give me your bindi.'

'Why?'

'I have to go for puja,' I say.

She smiles like an approving aunt and unpeels her bindi from her taut, brown forehead.

'Give me your mangalsutra also.'

Gangu-bai starts on how this black bead chain is not just an accessory, it is a lifeline, her husband's link to this world, her mark of respect as a married woman, and oh, okay, I can have her mangalsutra for two days of paid leave.

Only one thing left: I bring down the packet of tandoori masala from the kitchen shelf. I take a pinch of the angry red powder and streak it down my middle parting. It burns, it stings. But so does the necessity of festooning myself before approaching the State for assistance.

Looking somewhat like the perfect patni, I leave the house with my handbag tucked under my arm and my miya's photo inside it.

As always, all eyes on the street are on me. And, as usual, some lout tauntingly trumpets like an elephant.

'Sanpada Police Chowki,' I tell the autorickshaw driver. He shakes his head sadly and yanks at the start shaft.

I am glad the road is bad; the auto is forced to move at the pace of a sick snail. It allows me time to survey both sides of the street. I am still hoping to spot Sohail so I can abort the mission.

I haven't told anyone else; not his family, not mine. Outside of our private universe, Sohail and I wish to keep our dealings with others to the bare minimum. It helps that I work as an inconsequential graphic artist at an ad agency and Sohail is a medical transcriptionist. Now it is in this society, this world, that my Sohail has disappeared, leaving a gaping hole in the wall around our lives, so that strangers can stroll in and out, demanding passwords, threatening me with dire consequences.

'Something stolen?'

'What?' I look at the auto driver's reflection in the rear-view mirror. A trickle of sweaty masala dribbles down my forehead. I wipe it away with my handkerchief.

'You are going to the police station. So I was wondering if you have been robbed or something.'

I don my goggles to discourage any more small talk.

I have been robbed of my life—how about that, you nosy chap. Of the nineteen hospitals and three city morgues I telephoned, none claimed to have admitted a wounded, stabbed or dead man named S. Tambawala. I am afraid he could be lying in a gutter killed by a heart attack. Sohail is only twenty-nine, but he smokes too much. He says smoking is like belief in God—no real reason why, it just feels good. He worries I might get diabetes, but he has never asked me to lose weight. *Just die after I do, okay*, Sohail and I tell each other.

The driver turns on the radio. 'Please turn it off,' I snap. Thumping love songs would make me vomit on this most dismal rickshaw-ride of my life, made worse by the din of traffic and the dusty heat.

In the distance, the purple arch above the gate of Sanpada Police Chowki comes into view.

We are held up by a signal. I look around with a desperation only Sohail can trigger. Left, right: strangers and stray dogs.

Oh, Sohail, where *are* you?

A silly notion struck me last night: I became convinced Sohail had left me. I turned our flat upside down and swept the floor many times over in search of any goodbye note or memo that my husband may have written before setting off. I found nothing, of course. All of Sohail's belongings, including his toothbrush, are exactly where they should be. As I said, it was a silly notion. Because people like us, Sohail and I, we don't leave each other. All that coupling-up and breaking-off is for other people—other non-fat, non-smokers for whom the world is a pool of lovers from which to pick and choose.

The autorickshaw stops outside the police station. The driver refuses to take money. 'I'll pray for you,' he says, 'beshtofluck, haanh madam.'

Not good enough, my dear man. I need better luck than that.

I go through the wide-open gate and into a white-hot courtyard, like entering a nightmare in broad daylight. So this is how a police station looks, like an old Parsi bungalow, quaint and empty. Empty? Wait! Where is everyone?

I walk across the compound and up a short flight of stairs. The door facing the staircase is locked. Two other doors on either side are also locked. What is this, a police station or a mill on strike? Hello!

I walk up and down the veranda. I descend the stairs and look up, against the midday sun, at the two-storeyed building. Every window and door is hopelessly bolted.

Roop suhana lagta hai, chand purana... That disgusting film song. I look around. To my right, in the shade of a sprawling tree, I spot a lone havaldar slumped in a white plastic chair. *Tere aagey o jaanam*... It's coming from the red transistor pressed to his right ear.

'Excuse me!' I shout. The havaldar opens his eyes, blinks lazily (once, twice), and closes them. What cheek!

With my scalp marinating like chicken and my legs quivering like seaweed, I walk towards the world's most enthusiastic policeman. 'I said, excuse me! *He*llo!'

Shenior Conishtable Shegde

Yes, hello–hello. What hello–hello? What should I hello? Chi-aayeela! Cannot the fatty bambola see the station is closed? The lock on the door means CAL-O-SDA, closed. No one is here. Our dear PM is visiting this dangerous city so all policemen have gone for roadside duty. Except me. I am here because today is my last day. I am going to be dismissed from duty this evening.

Before leaving for bandobast, Inspector Chavan showed me the red file. 'Your dismissal orders are finally here,' he said. 'Stay back, relax, when I come back in the evening I will give you the discharge letter.' Chavan would not meet my eyes. Poor boy, I feel sad for him for feeling bad for me when there is nothing anyone can do.

Two weeks ago, three officers from Anti-Corruption Bureau caught me taking five hundred rupees from the owner of a Chinese food stall on Jamnadas Marg. They swooped in as Bittu was putting money in my shirt pocket. Bittu was more alarmed than me. 'I did not tell them, I did not tell them!' he kept shouting as the ACB snakes took me away for questioning.

I know Bittu did not tell them. The next morning I asked the cobbler, the popcorn seller, the batata-vada vendor, the paani-puri man—I did not threaten them; I just wanted to know who told ACB that I took money from everyone every month. '*We* did not do anything,' they all said. Yes, but who reported my name? '*We* did not do anything,' they kept saying like stupids.

It is okay; after Chavan returns this evening I will hand over my cap, my belt and my ID. In a few days I will join my brother's family in our village near Lonavala and request a security-guard job in one of the factories there. But I am worried for Gorya and Rajesh and Bittu. Junior Constable Dhodpode, the one who is going to replace me, is not like me. He is young and strict and too much of a policeman to tolerate sob stories from people doing business on the street illegally. He will tell them to pay the official monthly fine of two thousand rupees or get out and go do business elsewhere. I am most worried for Mohan, that legless, myopic, nearly mad newspaper seller; where will he go?

In the jeep, as the ACB men drove me to their office, I tried to talk to them, tried to tell them about the lives of people hawking on the streets. They have nowhere else to go. But no, I do not support what they do, so every month I try to break their backs a little, not by fining them the official two thousand rupees, but by taking what I know they can afford to give: five hundred from Bittu, three hundred from the two Rajeshes, hundred from Tukku Mama, and fifty from Kaliya, the mute coal seller. This way they remain where they are; they do not become bigger than their roadside selves and they do not become dangerous city scum.

'Sit shut!' one of the ACB men shouted at me. 'Shameless, corrupt man. Save these stories for the tribunal!'

I looked at the three ACB faces. They looked so grave and stern, more machine than human. Sometimes my replacement Dhodpode has a similar look on his face, upright and no-nonsense. I want to know: who are these new-generation officials?

What country do they come from? Arrey, do they not know that these petty criminals and roadside businessmen are our people only, we are just like them, how can we be so strict with everyone, how can we go about enforcing laws and ravaging lives like dictators? Policemen. We are police*men*.

'My, my,' said the Magistrate at the tribunal, 'now tell me, Senior Constable Shegde, if you feel so sorry for the illegal denizens of Jamnadas Marg, why do you take cuts from their meagre livelihoods every month?' I looked around the room in disbelief. Chi-aayeela, where was I? I felt like asking the Magistrate, this is India only, no? 'Everyone does it,' I said. 'Really?' the Magistrate said. 'Can you name your colleagues who take bribes?' Bastard. 'Everyone does it,' I repeated softly. The Magistrate huffed: 'Yes, and until we can afford to dismiss the entire police force and risk anarchy, I am dismissing *you*.' Two newspapermen in the room jumped to their feet shouting, 'Bravo! Bravo!' The Magistrate nodded humbly.

Bastards. We are not police for the rich and salaried only. We are also police for Nimmi the whore and Manilal the gutter-cleaner. Once Nimmi joked with me, 'Shegde, the day I get a license, you dare not ask me for money.' A customer told her that the government is thinking of giving licenses to sluts. Good, let them; and let them also give a permit to Umar-bhai for his barbeque-beef stand and an ID card to Bhanu-ben for her hooch shop. When all these people are respected by the government, so-called corrupt officials like me can run after real criminals who loot and murder. Question is, will there be any such criminals left?

'Excuse me, havaldar! I am talking to you!'

Deva rey, and now this woman. Educated people are always talking to *you*. I switch off my transistor. 'Station closed, madam. You go, come back in evening. Okay?'

The fatty acts shocked. 'What? How can a police station be closed?'

I look her over from top to bottom. Looks Indian, all right. Then why is she asking such mad-type questions? These people, these people are the problem. The police station must always remain open, the streets must always be clean, the neighbourhood must always be quiet. They pay a little tax and they think they can demand their own tiny country within the country. If it was an emergency, she would have dialled 100. Since she has decided to grace Sanpada Police Chowki with her bulk, I am sure she can wait till evening for the station to open. What can I do anyway? Tomorrow I will also be like her, a nobody, a civilian. Besides, did she not call me havaldar?

I get up from the chair under her shocked gaze and start walking to the barracks in the back. She follows me for a few steps, gurgling nonsensically, 'Havaldar…excuse me… I want to… I mean…havaldar…' Then she gives up.

Ah, finally some peace. These barracks were built the year before I joined service. See that fan hanging from the ceiling? The white one in the middle? A few years ago Pawar hanged himself from there. Fortunately, the fan survived. Pawar had joined service with me. Overly honest. He was strict with civilians— that, one could tolerate. But he was also lippy with the higher-ups, the inspectors and superintendents, asking them uncomfortable questions all the time. They kept Pawar Junior Constable; made me Senior after five years. But that's not why Pawar hanged himself. His wife ran away. What a fool, no? Is that something to kill yourself over? They say sometimes that fan starts on its own. I am sure Pawar is still around. 'Pawar?' I look up at the ceiling, 'Pawar, you are there?'

'Excuse me? Havaldar?'

Chi-aayeela! This lady has followed me here even! Look at her, filling up the entire entrance to the barracks. Good thing I did not strip to my underwear. 'Oh madam, I tell you no, station closed. Why you doing much-much? Go, come back in evening.' I start to close the door to the barracks.

'Please, please!' she says, and starts to cry.

Deva rey! Pinglé-madam should have been here. Junior Constabless Pinglé. Women can handle women well. What can a man do with a woman in tears? He is helpless.

'Tch, tch, what is this madam, why you are crying? Come, come in.' I lead her into the barracks and ask her to sit on a bench. I sit opposite her. 'Now tell me. What happened? House burgled, chain snatched, underworld called, what?'

She tells me.

My jaw drops. What? All this hassle for a runaway husband? Has she not seen herself in the mirror? 'You have his photo?'

She stops crying; smiles a little. She removes the photo from her purse and shows me.

Aaho, now I understand how the two got together. 'Good,' I say, 'what's his name?'

'Tambawala,' she says.

Yes, but that's a surname. What's her husband's *name*?

'S,' she says.

Is this any time to be coy? S? What S? Suraj, Sumit, Sudanshu, what?

'Sohail…'

What? 'Sohail? Like Sohail Khan, the actor?'

She nods, and then she says, 'But my name is Avantika.'

'You have some ID card or something?'

She looks more scared now. She tries to take back her husband's photo. *No, no*, I shake my head, *ID card first*. 'Show whatever you have. Bank card, ration card, anything.'

She brings out something from her handbag. 'My railway ID.' She gives it to me.

It's true. Name: Avantika Joshi.

'Why still Joshi?' I ask.

'My husband did not insist on a name change. He is very open-minded, very liberal. He even lets me wear sindoor and mangalsutra.'

I look closely at her head and neck. 'And he lets you go for puja also? To the temple?'

'Yes, yes, of course.'

She again tries to take back the card and her husband's photo. I pull them away and place them beside me on the bench. 'Which temple?' I ask.

Beads of sweat welt on her cheeks. What can I do? The effect of the khaki uniform is beyond my control. 'Haanh, madam? Which temple you go to?'

'…Siddhi Vinayak.'

Really? 'Which god you pray to?'

'…Krishna bhagwan.'

Krishna? What nonsense, there is no Krishna idol in Siddhi Vinayak. Every devout Hindu knows that.

I hand back her ID card and husband's photo. I stand up.

'Okay, madam, go, I will file the report.'

She looks up at me; she looks confused. 'Just like that? Don't you need more infor…'

'Yes, madam, this is Hindustan, not Arabastan. Everything happens like this only. You go now, okay?'

She gets up hesitantly. 'But…'

I join my raised hands with a loud clap. 'Arrey-aye, madam, enough! If you do not like it here, take your miya-ji husband and go to Pakistan.'

She leaves.

On That Very Same Afternoon

GK lay on his bed, arms and legs entangled with his lover's, their bodies so thoroughly enmeshed it was hard to tell them apart. The phone rang.

GK awoke, freeing himself from the snarl of limbs as his right arm reached for the receiver.

The caller was Balbir Pasha, the Assistant Commissioner of Police himself.

GK sat up. This had better be good. And it was. Balbir Pasha sounded nonchalant and to the point, like someone downplaying his own success, as he 'suggested' that GK get to Sanjay Gandhi Park 'if' he wanted to, because, well, the bodies wouldn't be around for too long, and the ambulances were already on their way, and GK could stay where he was if he didn't 'wish' to report how barely an hour ago Balbir Pasha and his unit had carried out one of the biggest ambushes on terrorists in months.

Rina, GK's lover, placed a hand on his bare back; GK shrugged it off.

Like all bastards with authority, Balbir Pasha was now revealing his inability to draw the line: he wanted GK to be at the park in fifteen minutes, cameraman and all; sorry, that was all the time he would allow before inviting rival news channels to cover the event.

GK wasn't intimidated. He only feared those whose price he

didn't know. Balbir Pasha's was three lakhs—the amount he had taken from Breaking News, GK's employer, in exchange for a promise to notify them first of any newsworthy event.

'I'll be there in an hour,' GK informed the Assistant Commissioner of Police.

And what were he and his men to do until then, Balbir Pasha asked. The bodies had begun to bloat, flies were descending in droves and, if he wasn't mistaken, he had even seen the MCBC news van prowling past the park looking for something to…

'Ballu, I said I'll be there in an hour,' GK reiterated. He wasn't afraid of sounding testy. GK had been there when Sir-ji, the sordid mogul who condescended to own Breaking News, had patted Balbir Pasha's cheek at a party and said, 'Ballu, look after us, yes?' and the Assistant Commissioner of Police had let loose a torrent of deferential ji-sirs.

GK smirked as Balbir Pasha hung up with the meekness befitting a Ballu.

Rina touched GK's bare back once again. GK leapt to his feet to flee this woman attempting to turn a straightforward one-night stand into something icky. Sex, like food, could be had any way, any time, appetite notwithstanding. But intimacy, like flavour, was an indulgence—and unfortunately for GK there were some faces he just couldn't see himself slobbering over.

'I got to go. You'll fax me the stuff, right?' GK asked directly and brazenly.

Rina thumped her head back on the pillow. 'Yeah, yeah, yeah.' Rina was a newspaper journalist working hard on the first big story of her year-old career—a story that she hoped would help rocket her standing, find her a well-placed husband and maybe, just maybe, bring down the state government. The day Rina's story broke, a few hours after copies of *India Informer* had been home-delivered to thousands of subscribers, Breaking News would air a detailed TV report on the story, anchored by GK, of course, while other newspapers and news channels looked about stupidly to make sense of this double whammy. Last night, while coordinating their joint efforts, it wasn't clear who had buckled under whose advances—or whether any advance had even been made. It was assumed that everyone would screw everyone, because that's how the news world was run—by a hyperintelligent, manic, sensualist population of bedfellows. Failing decency, the only way one could call upon others was by having fucked them—or at least their brains.

'No bye-bye kiss?' Rina called out.

GK froze at the door, horrified by this new request. 'Oh, okay,' he said and jerkily approached Rina, who cracked up laughing and began pointing at GK as if there were other witnesses to the scene.

'Pussy,' GK smirked, and turned around and left.

The Breaking News van picked GK up from the highway. The van was splattered with hundreds of inch-sized stickers of the Breaking News logo—a bluish white egg with a jagged crack running down its shell.

The channel had been around for over three years: people had ceased to find the not-quite-cracked-egg logo funny.

'You haven't shaved,' was the first thing Punita, the producer, noticed as GK boarded the back of the air-conditioned van. And in a few seconds more she had logged criticisms on GK's hair, his sweaty shirt, and the dark circles under his eyes. 'It's all going in my report,' Punita informed him. She handed GK a tube of foundation and a hairbrush. 'What's the lead?'

'Just a few hours ago, in a brave encounter, the Mumbai Police shot down X alleged militants holed up in Sanjay Gandhi Park. Assistant Commissioner of Police Balbir Pasha claims...'

'Enough,' Punita croaked. She was sick of this, all of this: driving around this shitty city for hours from riots to accidents, from one political briefing to another, one murder to the next, scampering around for news, breaking her head over link-up failures and studio screw-ups and asshole news presenters like GK who thought they were stars.

The van had entered the park spread over hundreds of acres of prime suburban land. The driver stopped to ask several people, who looked like they lived in the park, the location of the police—terrorist encounter. No one had heard a shootout, or anything about it.

Eventually, two policemen riding past on a motorcycle directed the Breaking News team to the scene of the encounter. 'See that forest?' the officer on the pillion seat pointed to a profusion of trees in the distance. 'Go in, drive towards your...your right, and you'll come across a small pond. Drive around it, and right behind a hillock you'll find...the, you know...'

Punita glanced at GK making last-ditch efforts to improve his appearance in the hand-held mirror. The two would have about ten minutes to gather information on the encounter, jot down a script and broadcast the breaking news for the nation's indifferent viewing. She ordered Girish, the cameraman-cum-technician seated beside the driver, to activate the satellite link-up.

GK looked to his producer. 'Fine?'

'Gorgeous,' Punita said without looking up from her laptop.

Fifteen. When GK learnt how many terrorists Balbir Pasha's unit had cornered and shot in the ambush, he smiled in spite of himself. Fifteen was a good number—not low enough to be ignored, not high enough to shock.

The Breaking News team, after walking past the barricade of police vans, arrived at the scene of the encounter.

Balbir Pasha was sitting on a stool, like a shikari, some yards from the corpses, all fifteen of which were laid out in a tight, neat row.

'Finally!' he cried out on seeing Girish, Punita and GK. He stood up and began pacing about. 'Come on, let's do this quickly. We have to take the bodies to the morgue.'

A gang of policemen converged behind Pasha, all of them staring googly-eyed at the Breaking News team. 'These are the heroes of the day!' Balbir Pasha pointed to the policemen. 'My fearless team. Are we going live?'

'Uh…ya…' GK managed to answer. He, Punita and the cameraman were transfixed by the row of bodies.

'We were tipped off by an anonymous caller this morning. I gathered my unit and we combed the entire park for two hours before we came upon this clearing where this bunch was sitting in a circle planning their attack on the prime minister. You know he's in the city for a week. My unit surrounded these jehadis from all sides. We wanted to capture them but they reached for their guns so we fired and finished the whole lot. It's a proud day for the Mumbai police force and a proud day for the country.'

Punita visualized the angle. Long shot? Overhead? Something zany or something still? She glanced at the bodies. Fly-infested. Mud-spattered. They were all dressed in shirts and trousers. Some had beards, some didn't. There were no pools of blood drooling from the carcasses. No remnants of gore. For men who had been shot just a few hours ago, these fifteen looked rather comfortable in their deadness.

Balbir Pasha pointed to an open trunk strewn with stick-like sten guns. 'AK-somethings,' he said. 'Our experts are still trying to figure out the make.'

And then Balbir Pasha went and stood by the head of the first corpse. 'We have their names,' he announced, referring to a clipboard. 'This one is Sohail Tambawala.'

And then he walked past each corpse and read out its name: 'Farid Khan, Rizwan Mohammad, Altaf Hussein Sheikh, Salim Itmadi, Irfan Shah, Rizwan Khambati, Munna Ismail…'

Punita's cellphone rang, interrupting Pasha's morbid name-calling.

'Really? Shut up! No *way*! This is *great*!'

Punita clicked her cellphone shut.

'We have to go.' She tapped Girish on his shoulder. 'Come on, we have to get to Santacruz.'

'What? But…' Balbir Pasha stuttered.

'What but, but! Prime minister slapped chief minister! We have to be there!'

The Breaking News trio returned to the van, slammed the doors shut and begged the driver to get them to Santacruz as fast as possible.

What Happened Next

The sight of the Breaking News van escaping at top speed stunned the Assistant Commissioner of Police.

Balbir Pasha imagined what it would be like if all nineteen news channels refused to report this police–terrorist encounter. There would be no media clamour for exclusive interviews, no public approval or disapproval, and no commission reports or judicial inquiries to divert himself with.

Like the director of a failed stage show, he would be left alone in this stinking park with his cast of twenty brain-dead officers and their gruesome props of fifteen rotting corpses.

The vision so terrified Balbir Pasha that he crumpled and fell to the ground, weeping like a motherfucking newborn.

What Really Happened Next

The sight of the Breaking News van escaping at top speed stunned the Assistant Commissioner of Police.

With expletives ricocheting inside his skull, Balbir Pasha dialled the first news channel that came to mind.

Studio staff at MCBC news were rather amused by the Assistant Commissioner of Police's desperate call for coverage. All field personnel had converged at Santacruz; would a rookie news team do?

'Send them! Send them!'

The MCBC News van arrived at the park.

In a matter of minutes the country's TV-owning population— the only one that really mattered—was regaled with a badly scripted eighty-second report on Balbir Pasha's heroics as well as his unit's stealth and precision. The names of the fifteen dead jehadis were ticker-taped.

As planned, the slap-happy prime minister incorporated the police–terrorist encounter into his rally speech.

Troublesome activists raised uncomfortable questions in comfortable living rooms.

Poll analysts predicted a second run for the ruling party.

Balbir Pasha was upgraded, like a desktop computer, to Joint Commissioner.

And in the same city, for the first time in their lives, several ordinary men grew conscious of their name, for they shared it with a dead terrorist—Sohail Tambawala.

Sohail Tambawala, 57

The death of a namesake is startling, like fate urging one to take note of a life, and death, that could have been one's own. And while one is incapable of empathy for anybody, leave alone anti-nationals, one finds oneself, in spite of oneself, reciting Surah Fatiyah for what could have been the soul of oneself.

Sohail Tambawala, 13

Tamby is what they call me at Light of Asia restaurant. I am a waiter there. There, the TV is on loud all day, placed on a stand facing the counter for the boss's exclusive viewing.

'Fifteen terrorists killed in an encounter...' the lady on TV announced one evening. When my name was broadcast, I was carrying a glass of tea to a man at table 3. '...Salim Itmadi, Sohail Tambawala, Altaf...' My gait staggered, my hand lurched and some tea spilled on the customer's little finger.

That night, with a face sore from being slapped, I stole *Dainik Saptah* from a news-stand. After the eleven other Tambys I share a room with had gone to sleep, I crept out to the stairs, spread the newspaper on the grimy floor, and searched. I found my name on page 2. Sohail Tambawala. He was dead as I am barely alive. A half-living terrorist waiter runaway small-town boy with stars in his eyes and bullets in his stomach. He, I, me, we—we were in the papers. *You're famous*, I whispered, striking a karate-chop pose on the rat-infested landing.

Sohail Tambawala, 42

Cosmopolitan hell demands that I reserve my cool, dress in my best and attend the Club party with my wife Zabia, where, as I am networking with three other businessmen as wealthy and disaffected as I am, Mrs D will swish by, offer her cheeks to our eager lips and coo, 'Sohail-bhai, did you read, that terrorist…?' 'Yes,' I will say. And she will say, 'Must be so embarrassing, to share a name with a terrorist!' And the air-conditioning will turn warm and my linen shirt will feel like wool and I will want, most of all, to stuff my goblet down Mrs D's gullet. 'Hey, hey, no bombs in here, okay!' Mr N will say, and he will exploit the bonhomie to touch Mrs D's desirable waist. 'I am not embarrassed,' I will say, pulling Mrs D against my body. 'I am happy. I think all those lower-class butchers and bhais and stinking bearded bastards must be shot dead for giving the community a bad name.' Mrs D will stroke, unseen, the back of my neck. 'Waawaaaah!' Mr T will lampoon the azaan and we will all laugh, a tad too loudly, till we choke on our whiskys.

Sohail Tambawala, 29

Lying on this hospital bed, with my smoker's lungs festering with cancer and a wife and family and reunited in-laws holding me back with their love—*you're too young to go*, Avantika says; *but one is never old enough to suffer like this*, I say—I read the papers and watch the news and wonder, will I be next? In the grand sweepstakes of death, will all Sohail Tambawalas be unlucky?

Sohail Tambawala, 20

Today it is a terrorist. Tomorrow it will be some enemy country's dictator. In the future, when a 'Sohail-dada' makes headlines, where will I hide my barrister face?

I want to become a lawyer, you see. I intend to apply to the Government Law College when the forms are distributed two months from now. My Business Communication professor says I am very good at presenting arguments. I said, 'Sir, aren't we all presenting arguments? Isn't every man a side of a debate?' Mr Solanki said not many people see things that way. You will do good, he said.

Not with a name like 'Sohail Tambawala'. With a name like mine I can only *hope* to do good. Who would have imagined a man's name to be his biggest enemy? Fed up, that's what I am. I want to do more in life than stand up for 'Sohail Tambawala' and the cultural maelstrom it implies.

'Sohail Tambawala' must go.

Tomorrow morning, on my way to the library, I will stop by at the Government Press office on Marine Drive. I will submit my Change Of Name form, pay the necessary fees and initiate the process of undoing history.

But change it to what? What will my new name be? I don't know yet. I am afraid of involving my parents or brothers in the decision. *Your roots aren't good enough for you*, they will say. *Go ahead, piss all over your ancestry! Get drunk, eat pork!*

For fuck's sake, it's just a name.

Isn't it?

I am in the bedroom, at my desk, practising future signatures in my notebook.

Rahul Vora.

Palash Roy.

Brij Desai.

I realize such things are rarely done—and rightly so—for they alter something fundamental, something untouchable. Already I can feel the shifting, like the preamble to an earthquake. I will not be Sohail Tambawala. Someday soon I will not be called Sohail Tambawala. How much more will I have to change? My laughter, too? And my taste in books and food, and pet fantasies of women with insanely large breasts? The pen slips; my palms have grown sweaty. This will be too much! Too disruptive! And apt, too, for the ethos I belong to, where there is no limit to the violence one may wreak upon oneself or on others—the chest beating at Moharram, the rigid observation of prayer time, the slicing of goat-necks by five-year-olds, the slicing of day-old penises.

You can't hear it; I can—the five o'clock azaan blaring from the mosque two buildings away; the grating of tiles from the shop across the street; and, till last Monday, deepening this daily cacophony were goats, eighteen of them, tethered to trees on the street, now dead and eaten and shat out by the collective arses of a people who have made life so much more difficult than it need be.

Jiten Mehra.

Yes, I think my new name will be *Jiten Mehra. Advocate Jiten Mehra. Jiten Mehra (LLB).* I bring out the Change Of Name form from my backpack. I have even acquired the form. I couldn't believe a thin porous sheet is all it takes to switch sides, to alter one's destiny. For the better? I would hope so. I am so excited I want to go to the Government Press right now and sentence 'Sohail Tambawala' to death. How many people know such delight! Or such anguish! To obliterate oneself. To birth a new self. Jiten Mehra will travel around the country freely; he will check into obscure hotels and not lie that he is Jayesh or Nimesh. One day, when he has become rich, he will move out of Yasin Baag to a cosmopolitan area. He will not see eyebrows rising (at police stations) or lips pursing (at railway counters) at the mention of his name. And when the electricity fails, Jiten Mehra will not wonder whether it's because of who he is or where he lives.

I practise my new signature. *Ji* merging into *ten* rising up to *Meh* breaking free with *ra*, a line back, a line forward. Astounding!

I'm ignoring much, I know. My address will still remain 32 Isaq Chambers. My father's name will still remain Barkatali. 'Sohail Tambawala' will always find ways to resurrect himself. How unfair to have to reduce one's existence to a political statement! Could I do it any other way? Probably. A wrong name here isn't as lethal as a wrong skin tone elsewhere. Or isn't it?

I place my head on the desk. What am I doing? At least some things in life must remain inviolate. I am a coward. I am being wise. I must stand by my roots. Must I sacrifice myself for my roots? And if 'Jiten Mehra' becomes a liability, will I obliterate him too?

I just want to be successful. I am too young to be ashamed of my ambitions. In the court, I want only my talent to matter—

not my name, not the hair on my face—just my ability to wrench justice from a system grown lethargic and rusty. There are two joys I foresee for myself: the winning of cases and the acquisition of comforts. And if 'Ngyn Mbuthe' would get me what I want, that's who I would become, that's how bad I want what I want.

My elder brother's wife enters the bedroom. I hide the Change of Name form. She can read English. 'What?' I ask.

She wants to know if I will do her a favour. Will I please go to the butcher's and get a two-kilo broiler? It's for dinner, she says. She's making Chicken Baghdadi for the family.

'Yes,' I say. Why not? A visit to the butcher! Crucial decisions must yield to inanity. I'll go.

Medina Chicken Mart is a street away from Yasin Baag— where I live—a ghetto of seven buildings and a mosque on the outskirts of a larger unruly Muslim inner city.

When I step out of Isaq Chambers, it is unbelievable how guilty I already feel. The three surrounding buildings are shaking their heads at me. The birds are fleeing from my aura. The mosque loudspeaker goes mute and, after I have passed, it returns louder, angrier, as if to cleanse the air of my name-changing toxicity.

I pass by my family's Maruti van parked on the street. My father and two brothers drive the Santro to our filter-paper factory. I walk past Shabir-bhai's shop; he is seated on a chair, contemplating air, oblivious to the worker beside him running a tile-cutting machine over a ceramic slab. In the flat above the din, through the clothes hanging at the window, I can see a woman bleaching her face. I pass by Inshallah-Mashallah Watch Repairers and nod at the grey-haired owner half-asleep in the evening swelter. Huddled around the tobacconist are my childhood friends, some of whose names I no longer remember, and all of who I know have nothing to do.

I cross the street (the footpath I was on is blocked by a grey heap of garbage which the municipality seems in no hurry to clear out). I cut across a gully. I am now on the parallel street. Squatting on either side of the road are hawkers, their wares spread before them like guts. Most are smoking. Everyone is spitting. And hovering over us all are the absurdly amplified screeches of the muezzin beckoning the faithful to prayers. In a hell like this, I guess God too must yell to be noticed.

A Honda City glides by. I am reflected in its windows. The revulsion on my face stuns me. And I am doubly stunned by the disgust on the face of the man *inside* the car, in the back seat, staring out at what must seem just another filthy Muslim ghetto.

'Catch it!' a man shouts.

A chicken sprints past me like a Bangladeshi jumping the border.

I am outside Medina Chicken Mart.

'Catch it!' a man shouts again.

I watch the chicken flee, but don't move an inch. No way am I going to obey some idiot and run after a bloody bird.

'Mooove!' Coming straight at me is a man in a vest and lungi with a cleaver in his hand.

I sneer and step aside.

Tomorrow morning I *will* go to the Government Press office and apply for my name change. Let someone else clean up this mess, which is disgusting no matter where one is—inside a luxury sedan, or outside on the stinking, noisy street. I just want to be a successful lawyer. Mahatma-dom can wait another fucking life.

'Moo…

Amjad, the Slayer of Lesser Life Forms

...oove!

Out of my way! If that chicken reaches the street, it will be crushed under some car or scooter. *I'll* have to pay forty rupees from *my* pocket while crows and cats enjoy a risky mid-road feast.

Where did he go? I check behind a hedge and inside cartons lying in front of APJ Paint Shop. I look under the cars parked nearby. Ah! Pukpukaak! Clinging to the axle of a Fiat, haanh? I drag the bird out by his wings. He yields to my grip. I hold him against my chest. A woman customer has selected this bird. As we approach the shop, the chicken starts to tremble. Crammed in the cage for three weeks, he has watched me carry his brothers and sisters to the back where I slash, de-feather, skin and chop them into pieces as per customers' orders. No wonder this chap wants to flee—he has observed and learnt to fear me.

'You sure you want this one only?' I ask the woman waiting outside the shop. The way I am hugging the bird, she says, 'Of course not, I'm not a monster! Give me another one.' Just as I am about to put the freedom fighter back into the cage, a youth standing next to the woman says, 'I'll take it, I'll take that bird!' I say, 'Are you sure? This one?' My boss Jamal Seth says, 'Of course he's sure! Just give the customer what he wants!' I shrug. Just a butcher.

I take the chicken to the back of the shop and press its quivering neck on the chopping board. It croaks, like a person choking on life. Man and beast become identical when death looms—no one wants to die.

I know. I have killed men.

Medina Chicken Mart is a halaal shop, not some sinful jhatka-house like those Sikhs have up north. Here, I slice chicken-necks while reciting Quranic verses till the blood drains away and the bird has stilled. Why? So realization dawns on the bird as it meditates on its death. Mostly, though, the chickens meditate on me. As the blood escapes their gullets, they stare with such disappointment in their beady eyes that I feel like quitting and becoming a fakir. But I don't have a choice; who will feed my parents, my wife and our son? He is two years and nine months old. Doesn't speak yet. Only gurgles and grins at everything like a simpleton. 'Genetic damage due to excessive inbreeding,' the doctor had said while shaking his head in horror, because my wife is my aunt's daughter, my father is my mother's uncle, and my wife's mother and father are first cousins. Whatever. My son will improve as he grows. Allah is great.

A chicken's heart beats even outside its body. I never knew that till I came to work here. In the beginning, just for fun, I had thrown a chicken's heart on the floor and watched the purple kernel-shaped chunk pulsate and wriggle about, leaving a red trail like a snail. After some minutes it stopped suddenly, accusatively. I was overcome with such grief—as if the chicken's soul, in passing, had cursed me. Since then, I put the heart with the body or fling it in the bin behind me.

Every two months, coinciding with the breeding habits of

chickens, the price of their meat goes above rupees fifty per kilo Customers prefer mutton or beef. No one enters the shop. I sit and stare at the livestock. What else to do? The cage has five levels. The chickens in the top row are fresh arrivals. They come from the farm in a round wicker basket, twice a week, ten at a time, clean and calm and unsuspecting. They gape like awe-struck villagers, not understanding why the old-timers in the racks below are so noisy and difficult. As they begin their row-wise descent to death, these new chickens, worn out by heat, fear and lack of space, gradually become restless and cranky, till at last they turn so unlovable as to deserve to die. I get attached to a bird at times; if it is especially comical or very weak like my Ziad, I keep it aside till Jamal Seth spots it in the cage and wonders why it isn't being offered to customers. He is sly; keeps an eye on everything, with a handkerchief perpetually pressed over his nose. Customers wink at me. 'Where's your Murgh-e-Aazam?' they ask when Jamal Seth isn't around. He is hardly ever there.

It is I who opens Medina Chicken Mart in the morning. On arriving, I step out of my shirt-pant and hang them on a nail high above the bloodiness below. I put on my uniform, then— a blue chequered lungi and netted vest. My friend Mushtaq had said that in these clothes, with the cleaver in hand and black amulets around my right arm and neck, I look like an *asli kasai*, absolute butcher-man. Jamal Seth had admired his wit.

Now Mushtaq doesn't even know when to shit. He has been circling the city yelling mother-sister abuses for eight years, ever since his laundry-cum-clothes-rental shop at Anjeerwadi was gutted by neighbouring slum-dwellers. It was the night after the masjid was broken. The night people stopped being neighbours, cobblers, tailors, bakers, vendors or drivers, and everyone turned Hindu or Muslim, Hindu against Muslim. It was the night some Hindus wished they weren't Hindu and most Muslims wished they weren't Muslim. When the curfew lifted three days later, Mushtaq rushed out like other anxious businessmen. He searched Anjeerwadi for his shop, not finding it where it should have been, as if shops could be mislaid. He ran in and out of the slum's gullies, refusing to believe that *that* fifteen square feet of ashen heap was his shop. He has been searching ever since, refusing to believe. On spotting Mushtaq running by, I catch him by his grimy collar and drag him to a food stand where I feed him enough to last a day. Who knows when I'll see his crazed face again?

I used to give my lungi and vest to Mushtaq for washing; no one ever asked to rent them, of course. Now a dhobi, a bhaiya from UP, launders my clothes and demands five rupees extra to ignore the gore, the stink.

It drives my wife Laila up the wall and over the roof. 'Why pay that dhobi extra? What am I here for? I'll wash your clothes!' she says. But I refuse to let her. 'Then tell your Jamal Seth to pay the dhobi. Why should we?' she asks. At twenty, Laila understands nothing. How can I be petty over ten rupees for laundry when, in addition to my monthly salary of two thousand, Jamal Seth allows one free chicken every week? I take it home for the family. No thanks, no chicken for me. Since I began working here, I cannot stand aromas in my food. So no chicken, no onions and no garlic. My meals consist of boiled vegetables. If my food asserts itself at all, I vomit. If Laila applies perfume, I thrash her. Like bakers who reek of biscuits and chemists who stink like alcoholics, the stench of chicken guts and feathers has possessed me. I avoid all other smells. To be comfortable with discomfort, one must banish all contact with ease. She is a great woman, my Laila, my queen. Only once has she repelled me: On our wedding night, when I sprung up and hugged her, she breathed in and vomited the rich wedding food on our flower-strewn bed. Now the same girl offers to clean my foul, feather-flecked lungi and vest!

Yet, there is something even my Laila seems to have an everlasting aversion to: cockroaches. She screams at them as if they are mosque-wreckers. Like on sighting a rat in the shop, Jamal Seth lifts his feet off the floor and yells, 'Amjad! Choohaa! Maar usko!' They expect me to kill them. Cockroaches—okay, they are like brown smelly wisps of air. But Bombay's rats are big as cats; killing them is like killing a person. People think butchers can kill anything. It's one thing to kill for money like I do at Medina Chicken, like executioners and assassins do; killing for money shows a desire for good things, a better life. But to kill out of hatred or fear hardens the heart. I have done my share of such killing and want no more. With the wooden handle of my cleaver I rap the rats on their furry little skulls and kick them to the walkway outside.

Medina Chicken Mart is part of a market. There is an open gutter at the market's entrance (this is where rats breed whole generations). Our great muncipaltee, instead of fixing the gutter, put planks over the four-feet-deep sewer so people can cross over.

One evening some months ago, a drunk slipped into this

gutter. No one dared to help. He languished for twenty minutes amid dead fish from the pet shop, phlegm from the grocer's chest, curdled white slush from the milkwallah, blood from Medina Chicken and litre upon litre of piss from all of us. When the fire brigade came for him, there was a huge audience.

The man, as it turned out, was headed for Medina Chicken Mart. And he was not drunk, just short-sighted. After being dragged out of the muck, he proceeded to weave through random passageways of the market and halted outside MCC to read the board above our entrance.

We smelled him—Jamal Seth and I—before we saw him. A heady, lukewarm odour of the sludge that drains unseen below the city. *This smell*, I thought as I rinsed the cleaver, *I could get used to even a smell like this.* Jamal Seth tightened the handkerchief over his nose. 'Are they cleaning the gutter this time of the evening?' It was one of the few evenings Jamal Seth hadn't already left.

Then we saw him—a short sodden figure outside the shop. He was bleeding black filth from the waist down. Passers-by took difficult detours to avoid being near the man, keeping the space around him magically empty. Entranced, I did not notice that he had begun moving towards the shop.

'Abbey hutt! Amjad, tell that thing to stay away! Shhoo! Hutt!' Jamal Seth stamped his feet and motioned as if at a crazed animal. The man stopped some feet from the entrance and grinned at my boss's histrionics. My heart warmed to the stranger—he stank worse than me and found my boss amusing.

'What do you want?' I asked.

'What do you mean what do you want? Just drive him away!'

Jamal Seth shouted again. He rolled a newspaper and threatened to strike the stranger with it.

The man raised his hand. 'I don't want to enter your shop, okay,' he said. 'Just, which one of you is Amjad Farsi?'

Jamal Seth looked at me.

'What happened to you?' I asked the man.

'I fell in the gutter.'

We crumpled our noses.

'Don't laugh. Allah has made me short-sighted. Are you mocking Allah's actions?' the man said. 'Who is Amjad Farsi?'

'I am. Who are you?' I was smirking.

'Wasim Sheikh's brother,' the man said.

'Who?'

'You don't know my brother?'

'No,' I said.

The man patted his head as if to calm himself. 'You kill a man and don't even remember him?'

'What did you say?' Jamal Seth squinted.

The man pointed at me, 'He! He killed my brother! He also killed my brother's friend!'

Jamal Seth turned to me. 'What? What's he saying, Amjad?'

I tightened my grip on the wooden handle of the cleaver. 'You've gone mad,' I said.

'Have I?' the stranger said. The sludge had formed a puddle around his feet.

'When did this happen?' Jamal Seth asked. Above the handkerchief, his eyes were probing like roach antennae.

'Ask him yourself, why don't you?' the man said, crossing his hands over his filthy torso. They both fixed their gazes on me—

twin beams of vengeance and disbelief. I stared at an uneven tile protruding from the pavement outside the shop.

'Amjad? What is this man saying? You killed his brother?' Jamal Seth asked.

A slight shake of my head was enough for my boss. He turned to the stranger. 'Don't waste our time with this nonsense. Get lost. You're mistaken.'

'I know he remembers! Unless he kills men every day, he can never forget taking those lives. Ask him! Force him to speak. Why he is standing like a dummy? It was in March, at Tupalgam village. He killed my brother and two other men,' the stranger said.

Jamal Seth looked at the stranger, then at me. 'If it's true, why isn't he in jail?'

The man fanned out a black hand. 'Who will arrest him? They themselves kill Muslims. What, they'll arrest a Muslim for killing Muslims? My brother's death isn't even recorded. But I know. I found out. Birth and death are too big to remain hidden. This man killed my seventeen-year-old brother! Had he been a Hindu I would have hacked his neck by now. But when one of us is at fault, what to do? *What to do?*'

What? I gaped at the muck-drenched man standing outside Medina Chicken Mart. What was he talking about? Why did everything have to be about religion?

Which one was Wasim Sheikh anyway? The one kissing the girl or the one kneading her bare buttocks? To think would have been a sin. There was my hand lifting a nearby brick. There was the brick in my hand. There was the brick coming down with two sure strokes. There were the two men, now dead, their skulls split open by the brick. There was the girl lying on the grass. A dumbfounded eight-year-old. I picked her up. She was trembling like a chicken. She led me to her hut. I handed her to her parents who knew nothing of where their child had just been, or how close she had come to becoming a woman. There had been thanks given and tears sobbed. The girl's clan members followed me to where the two men lay. There had been assurances given of silence. It was the night I had gone visiting Laila's parents at their village. The night I had gone strolling after dinner and heard the girl's sobs coming from a dark, wooded spot. For once it had nothing to do with who I was, what I did, or Whom I revered. It was simply about two perverts, a low-caste girl and a butcher who did what he had to do.

'Amjad, this has gone too far. What is this man saying? And don't just shake your head, you hear me? Speak!' Jamal Seth huffed. 'I won't have a man working... I mean, I want the truth!'

I curled my lips. 'It's time to close. I have to go pray.'

I placed the cleaver on the bloody tabletop. Under the gaze of the two men, I washed my limbs, changed into my shirt-pant, and combed my hair in the tiny mirror on the wall.

Jamal Seth barred my way, 'Come on, Amjad. Answer this man.'

I guided my boss aside by his soft shoulder, 'You must not stop me. It's time for namaaz.'

The stranger stretched out his arm. 'No, you cannot go without saying. Why you killed my brother, you butcher? Why? Why you killed him? What he did to you?'

As I neared the man on my way out, his stench made my legs

wobble. But I pressed onwards, against and past his outstretched arm. The muck on his sleeve rubbed off on my shirt. There was now a black blot on my chest smelling like hell itself. I was wrong: I could never get used to a smell like this. Would Laila offer to clean this as well? How much more would the dhobi charge to ignore this new filth? For the first time in three years I stumbled through the passageways of the market looking to douse myself with attar or spices or turpentine—anything to mask the stench of me.

Jamal Seth, the Desperado

There is a limit to how much ugliness a man can bear. I am afraid I have reached my breaking point for today. Medina Chicken Mart closes at eight p.m. It is five right now. I am already restless. I have been here since twelve noon. With a handkerchief pressed over my nose like a gora sahib, I have been going through the motions of business. A customer once asked me whether my handkerchiefs are perfumed. I ignored the insinuation. If I get used to the smell of chickens, what next? How many more of my senses will I have to deaden for the sake of practicality? So although this chequered square of cotton does little to bar the stench from my nostrils, and although I am losing the respect of customers, the handkerchief will remain— like a last vestige of my humanity, or whatever little of it is left.

I sit at a counter at the front of the shop, facing the walkway outside. To my left is the cage of chickens. Beside it sits Amjad, my employee butcher. Surrounding us is the soupy, vibrating stinkstenchsmell of the birds. We have had an especially good afternoon today. Eleven units. Chickens sometimes aged and died in the cage itself—but that was in my father's time. Now non-vegetarianism is epidemic. As are lies, treachery, murder, promiscuity and heartlessness. No one knows what is right or wrong. Is it wrong to be the owner of a chicken shop? Wrong to oversee the butchering of twenty to thirty birds every day?

And then to make money out of this? Is all this wrong? Really, I really want to know. But who's going to tell me? Five youths in Save Earth T-shirts had picketed the shop once. Non-vegetarianism, they said, is wrong. Must I close my shop, I asked. They didn't know. 'We're here to sensitize, not propagate,' one of them said, and round and round they went in circles outside my shop, chanting jingles that extolled the virtues of vegetarianism. I almost joined them, enthused as I was by the spirit of those teenagers, till I remembered I was the enemy.

My attention strays to the wall above the cage where an old clock smoulders with time. Seventeen minutes past five. I would like to walk out this very instant. But sometimes I like torturing myself. At least this much I know is wrong. To torture oneself is wrong. *Anything that makes a man happy is right. Anything that makes a man unhappy is wrong.* But what is a man to do when something makes him neither happy nor sad? Most of the time I feel nothing. The propriety of my actions remains unknowable, and my attempts to ascertain right from wrong resembles a blind man opinionating on colour. I wonder: is it like this with everyone? Does Amjad *feel* anything as he slaughters away to glory from morning to night? Did he *feel* anything when he killed those two men? I don't know for sure whether he did, I don't *want* to know, but assuming he did, did Amjad feel anything while taking human lives? I do not think so. The feelings are missing. They have vanished. What's left are instincts, sensations, drives and passions. Inside, everything is dead.

The evening's first customer enters; I know him—a freelance chef who caters to parties in the neighbourhood. Things will get busier as night approaches. I am glad I will not be around then. The man ignores me and approaches Amjad because—because it is the kink of modern commerce: the doer owns nothing, the owner does nothing. Amjad comes to the counter and whispers, 'Jamal Seth, customer wants a discount. He wants thirty kilos.' I declare a five-rupee holiday per kilo. The caterer agrees. The genocide begins.

I am off. It is five-thirty. I stand up and push back my chair. Amjad is carrying the first four chickens, two in each hand, to the back of the shop. 'I'm off,' I say, 'see you tomorrow.' He waits for my exit. I remove a thousand rupees from the cashbox, blood money, and have to restrain myself from breaking into a run. This place augments the income of my family of two parents, sisters and a freeloading cousin. I cannot sit through all its working hours. The least I can do is *walk* away. I walk away. And when the stench is no more to be seen (yes, sometimes it is so thick, I can see it), I stuff my handkerchief in my trouser pocket and head straight for my bike in the market's parking lot.

Outside of Medina Chicken Mart, and because of it, my leisure hours are devoted to the tracking and hunting down of beauty in all its squirming, reluctant forms. Money and mobility are essential to the endeavour.

Kickstart...and...vroom.

I have been motorcycling since sixteen. I suffocate in other modes of transport. I am the man you see hanging out of train doors or being air-blasted on upper-level front seats of double-deckers. I walk; if being boxed-in is the only way to get somewhere, I do not go. I see no merit in flexibility. Yield, and soon your whole world is gone.

My buddies are wondering what we should do tonight: dinner

in the ghetto or gatecrash a college jam session? I have joined them on the footpath outside a grocery store that has served as our meeting point for several years, sometimes to the chagrin of the owner, sometimes to his relief and delight. This evening, since we have all ordered colas and cigarettes, the grocer is gracious. I have three friends I shall not name. We are all the same: except for some details (one of my friends is an orphan, the other almost a dwarf, the third can speak fluent English) and varying livelihoods, I would be hard-pressed to assign unique personalities to any of us. We are a pack, a herd. Think of us as one. In these few hours of bonhomie, we regain the vigour sapped through the day. We sit on our bikes and gossip or talk business. Sometimes we play cricket with makeshift apparatus. When we're bored, we brawl. For men in their late twenties, we are alarmingly incapable of stillness. When I sleep, even my dreams are action-packed.

Two of my pals have had a windfall in their lines of work; they want to do something extraordinary this evening. This is just talk, of course, because our itinerary varies as predictably as the days of the week. Still, something special must be done. We settle on a dance bar. In a suburb, along the National Highway, is a new place called Samudra Mahal. One of us had been there a few nights ago; he sings such paeans to the pleasures to be had there, we decide to set off at once. With the lives we live, it's never too early or too far to watch half-naked women gyrate. The two cash-rich ones agree to shoulder most of the expenses. Samudra Mahal. Beautiful women shaking their goods for me. My crotch pulsates in anticipation. Thanks to AIDS and concomitant diseases, the dread of which public campaigns have successfully instilled in people like me (the middle class, ever ready to heed alarms), our eyes are now our cocks, and to ogle is to hug, kiss, fondle, undress, mount and fuck, all rolled into one.

The pack is on the move. Four motorcycles weaving in and out of lanes, racing, swerving, overtaking from the left. The promise of sleaze makes us reckless. We leave in our wake shaken motorists and a traffic flow made fragile by our passage. At least we have been noticed, even if for the disruption we have caused; for the chronically powerless, this is revenge enough.

We ride past a girl in shorts and, because we have no words to compliment her sexiness, cannot help propagating a stereotype embraced unquestioningly and are afraid to approach her, the four of us honk. The girl turns her head. I look back and wink. She widens her eyes. I accelerate to catch up with the others. 'Uttha lein?' one of us shouts over the roar of traffic. We laugh. But this is no joke for me. The abduction of a girl is a tempting course of action. Not to rape and discard the abductee, but to detain her long enough to win her affection. Half a chance to impress is all I ask for. I cannot remember the last time I spoke to a girl I was not related to, someone I could amuse with my Amitabh Bachchan imitation. We would talk, I would ask about her likes and dislikes, birth sign, and then I would propose. Why can't my sisters hurry up and get married? Being the elder brother, I must wait till both have wedded. My sisters, however, seem in no hurry to say 'yes' to any one of the thousands of boys we have shown them. How did they grow so willful under their burkhas? Some of us do not want to wait for perfect loves and ringing bells. Some of *us* are tired of honking at girls and driving across town to watch sluts dance. Will someone please tell my sisters that some of *us* just want to get on with our bloody lives!

We are too early. Pig-guts! In our mad-monkey rush for illicit thrills, we have completed in an hour a journey that should have taken at least twice as long. It is eight p.m. Samudra Mahal has not even opened. The sign above the dance bar is still unlit. Damn! There are waves around 'Samudra Mahal'; the 'S' is a topless mermaid stretching with an erotic lethargy. All this would have looked *so* good in neon.

Some place else, then? No. The one who suggested this place is angry. He goes to ask when it will open.

He comes back grinning: the place is open. There is no electricity, but it will be back in some time. No, he will not allow us to go elsewhere. *Please*, he pleads with the other two, for they have promised to pay for this evening, *the women in here are to die for*!

Okay, okay. We park our bikes. We backslap and kick each other as we approach the entrance. For men in their late twenties, we are worryingly juvenile.

These are moments I relish: transitional moments, when the tedium of the day and the promise of pleasure just minutes away are both pressingly real. I can still smell the shop on my clothes. But I can also already imagine the smell of smoke inside the dance bar and the flavours of appetizers drifting on drafts from the air-conditioning. The cage will be replaced with a stage; the poop-streaked grilling with disco lights; the chickens will turn into bar girls dressed in clothes revealing cleavages and midriffs. The girls will be smiling, their bodies moving in sync to whatever dissonance is currently parading as music. I will, as usual, fall in love with one of the dancers and convince myself that *she*, as against the others, is chaste and innocent. Such moments make me happy; they have got to be right.

I, because I am ahead—ever the eager beaver—go first through the wooden door of Samudra Mahal, watched by two guys in neckties and a bearded man. There is an unlit passage behind the main entrance. What is it? Something does not feel right. In passages like these the day should begin to shrivel, and the night should awaken like a woman from deep slumber. This passage is too warm, too silent. Past the passage, I push open a tinted glass door. No! Of course! It's the electricity. There's no electricity! 'Let's go elsewhere, boss, come on!' I say to my friends, I insist, and turn around to leave. But the other three do not want to be bothered. 'This will be no fun,' I say, 'let's go, boss, please!'

Three emphatic NOs.

The restaurant is hot, silent and dark, except for two tube lights burning on battery. Conversations stop when we enter. Eyeballs rotate. The air is sagging like an overloaded clothesline. Too many things have been suspended in here.

Three tiers of tables are arranged in a semi-circle facing a raised platform. On one side of the room, around one tube light, sit a group of women and men. The four of us sit on the opposite side, around the second tube light, where five other men are already seated. Employees and clients. These battery-operated tube lights are made in China. I can tell. Their gloss and curved contours cannot conceal the cheeky smile of fraudulence. A battery-operated fan has been directed at us. Touching.

We know we have merged with the scenery when a woman giggles and breaks the silence. Conversations resume, but only among the employees. We clients are too busy stealing glances at the dancers. They seem fantastical in the dim light. Depending on how they are facing the tube light, only parts of their bodies are illuminated: someone's left cheek, someone's arm, someone's mirror-studded bustier. The talk is ribald. A woman is being teased for something she swears she did not do. Another woman has a fever. A man is on the phone ordering ice.

What nonsense! We should not be seeing and hearing all this. I want the finished product. Those breasts should be in motion. The one in the white halter-top—her hair should be strewn over her undulating shoulders. And why am I still thinking? The lights and loud music ought to have stunned me by now.

They should have kept the doors sealed. The wait would have made us hungrier. But to allow us in like this, and to seat us here in the dark, is to replicate the tedium that we have come in here to escape.

Fuckers, I whisper, *let's just go somewhere else, this is depressing.* At least one of my friends agrees. The other two are not so sure.

I stand up. I am alone. Now all three are not so sure. *Fuck ya'll*, I say, and move towards the door.

'Sir, sir!' A man in a waiter's uniform comes running. 'What's the problem, please wait, lights will come on any moment, don't go, sir!'

I want to smash the bastard's nose for drawing everyone's attention to me. 'No, no,' I say, 'I'm going, I can't waste my night waiting for your bloody lights.'

'Arrey, sir, don't be angry na,' a woman says. I look past the waiter's shoulder. A bar girl is winding her way to me. Her black sari is hitched way below her navel, her white sleeveless blouse is cutting into her flesh. So what if the light is dim, I am a bat where these things are concerned.

'Sit na, sir, please, don't go.' The bar girl is yanking me by the hand. The touch of her soft palm floods my loins. She is not young. My bat eyes fail to ascertain her exact age, but I can tell from the rotundity of her upper arms that the woman has been around longer than any of the girls.

I yield to her tugging. I am pulled to the tables and seated with the other clients.

'This is for you, dear,' the bar girl says.

She turns to her colleagues and claps a rudimentary beat. The other girls whoop and giggle. Then they too start clapping— like gypsies around a campfire, like eunuchs, like soft-spoken women calling out to someone far, far away. Clap. Clap, clap.

The bar girl turns to us clients. She hooks the loose end of her black sari into her skirt.

And then she starts—to my utter embarrassment, in the near darkness, to the simple beat of hands clapping—to dance.

Whistles go up from the clients' side.

'*Chhaawee!*' two men cheer.

The bar girl places one hand on her hip, the other on her head, and begins twitching and lurching. She jumps from foot to foot. She twirls, prances, hops, jiggles her breasts and then her buttocks, all to the sound of hands clapping.

I have been re-seated at the very front, away from my friends, with no face-saving distance between the girl and me.

The men seated behind me pat my shoulders. One man flashes the thumbs-up sign at me.

I loosen up. I start to savour the impromptu performance. My eyes turn frantic, trying to take in as much as possible. My dick turns half-hard and will remain so all through the evening.

The man on my right sticks two fingers in his mouth and blows a shrill whistle. And one more. And one more. 'Phhhhiissst…phhhhhissstt…phhhhhisssssstttt!'

The clapping turns synchronized.

The bar girl's movements take on a fresh vigour. As she shimmies on the floor, her movements become affected, louder, the sweep of her limbs turns wider, her steps go from suggestive to farcical.

A hesitation descends upon us clients. The cheers and whistles die down. What the…

The girl is not quite dancing any more. She swaggers about like a drunk. She twitches like an epileptic. Lurches. Marches around like a soldier. Rolls on the floor. Slaps her own face. Paces back and forth like a tigress. *Huh*?

Then she starts beating her own chest. Whack! Whack! She paces the floor and beats her chest. The other girls continue to clap like machines. Thuck! Thuck! The bar girl rolls on the floor again. She stands up. Leaps into the air. Slaps herself again. Grabs her private parts.

Two clients stand up.

But of course!

The clapping falls to pieces, a staccato mess. A waiter comes running—the same one who had stopped me from leaving.

'Tell her to stop this madness,' one of the men who have stood up says to the waiter. 'What's this nonsense!'

The bar girl stops. She just stops: with her right hand on her groin, and her left hand clutching her behind. 'Why? What happened? You didn't enjoy?' the girl asks.

The two men do not answer. They storm past the bar girl

and approach the entrance. The waiter tries to stop them. The two customers are adamant. The waiter grabs one of them by the arm. In response to this gesture of friendly insistence, he— the waiter—is rewarded with a punch on his right shoulder and a laser beam stream of abuses. *Sisterfucker. Son of a whore. Pimp!*

I squirm in silence. What have I started!

And what did the woman think she was doing?

Our eyes meet. Because I am closest, and the light is dim, only I can see the bar girl's malicious smile. She flicks her eyebrows at me.

What? What's with all this? The defiance on her face. The hostility. Is she *angry*? Why is *she* angry? She was the one who stopped me from walking out. She offered to dance. And then she was the one who made a complete fool of herself. And now why is she flicking her eyebrows at me? And why this baring of teeth? I did not force her to do anything. I thought she was happy to dance for us. If she was not, why did she volunteer?

I get up and join my friends in the rear row.

I am greeted with much backslapping and whispered *well dones*.

I try to come up with smart retorts. I try to laugh. But it is so dark back here. And wherever I look, I can see the bar girl's bitter stinging smile superimposed onto the darkness.

This is not fair. It is really not.

She should not dance if it makes her unhappy. Someone should tell the bar girl that. Someone should tell her that it is wrong to do something that makes you unhappy.

And now I have the rest of the evening—a whole evening— to take joy in someone else's unhappiness.

The Rest of the Enjoyable Evening

The two customers who had walked out of the bar returned.

They were followed by two men in neckties and an obese bearded man, the bar owner: the three men whom Jamal Seth had encountered while entering Samudra Mahal.

On learning why the two customers had left the establishment, the bar owner requested the two not to go: *Come, come inside with me, I'll look into this*.

As the group walked back in to the shadowy premises, one of the walkout customers yelled at the bar owner, 'Did we say anything? Did we mind waiting for the lights? Then why did she have to insult us with that circus? Dancing like that. As if we have no sense of what looks nice!'

Jamal Seth wished he could disappear; he knew where this would go.

The bar owner demanded to know which girl had danced like a monkey.

Shakila, the one in the black sari and white sleeveless blouse, stood up. 'What do you mean?' She stormed over to the owner. 'With no lights or music, I tried my best! What else could I do anyway? He…' (and here Shakila pointed to Jamal Seth who was, for all practical purposes, *dying*), 'he was about to walk out! He said he couldn't waste his night waiting for our bloody lights!'

The owner glanced at the junior manager who had been in the bar all along.

The junior manager confirmed Shakila's version of the fracas with a nod.

Because she had done nothing wrong—ostensibly, at least—Shakila ceased to matter. Mankind closed its ranks, crowding the bar girl out.

The bar owner embraced the two walkout customers. He requested them to sit down again, forget about what just happened, would they like a beer, free beers for all nine customers kind enough to wait for the power. The bar owner forced a handshake with Jamal Seth, joked with him: sweet are the fruits of patience, etcetera, etcetera. The beers were not ice-cold when they arrived. But because they were free, none of the customers protested.

Another group of men entered Samudra Mahal.

There was a sudden crackle in the air. A sudden hiccup of the air-conditioning and a premonitory flicker of the lights.

Male voices buzzed with approval when the electricity returned to the bar.

The music snapped to life: a jolt of treble and bass that made the floor rumble.

More patrons entered.

The bar girls emerged from the dressing room after touching up their make-up and adjusting their costumes that had wilted in the heat and the dark.

The seven bar girls, dressed differently to suit the varied tastes of patrons, filed on to the dance floor.

The music bypassed their minds and hearts and spoke to

their bodies. Their bodies started to respond. A twitch here. A sway there.

'Come on ladies, we don't have all night!' a manager shouted.

The bar girls started—breasts and buttocks moving up-down up-down with robotic precision. Hands jogging, heads swinging, their long black hair whipping each other's faces. Beams of blue, red and orange strobe lights dissected the dance floor. The first gust of air-conditioning chilled the dancers' sweat-drenched blouses. Customers' gazes darted across the barroom and clung to the women's bodies like bats. The music intensified. Waiters ran about with glasses of alcohol and buckets of ice and plates of roasted meat...

Much Later That Night

A taxi carrying a lone female passenger was zipping through empty streets, past shuttered shops and footpaths strewn with sleeping tramps.

The breeze was soggy. Summer's heartbeat had quickened. As usual, the vibe of monsoon had arrived long before its official date of onset.

At a crossroad, the taxi driver was forced to stop in deference to a water tanker making a laborious U-turn.

A grubby, ghastly beggar, meaning to try his luck one last time at the end of a luckless day, arose from the footpath and approached the taxi. He beseeched the lone woman in the back seat to spare some change.

The woman, with her cheeks aching more than her legs (for more than the dancing, it was the simulation of delight that exhausted her every evening), suppressed her philanthropic instincts. Tonight, she let her hands lie limp on her handbag, containing four hundred and sixty rupees in denominations of ten, earned as tips from customers.

The beggar rested his hands on the edge of the taxi's window.

The woman would dole out nothing. Neither would she touch her forehead and beg the beggar's forgiveness. Tonight, she wouldn't even look at his kind.

'Aye, memsaab, in god's name, give some money for food'

and other such age-old appeals had no effect.

The woman lifted her hand. The beggar grew hopeful. The woman groped around for the pedal on the inside of the taxi's door. She wound it clockwise and, with each revolution of the pedal, the transparent window rose bit by bit like a flag.

The beggar retracted his hands.

The woman had walled herself inside the taxi, her eyes set stonily on the road ahead.

The beggar turned around and walked back to the footpath. He lay down under a bus stop. The taxi sped away behind him.

He regretted having tried at all. What a waste of precious energy. The beggar believed he had received *nothing* from the woman in the taxi.

He was wrong.

He had been given. The virus transmitted. The score settled.

The woman in the taxi had made the beggar—a *man*, a representative of his detestable kind—endure the agony of his own insignificance.

(Not that it amounted to much.)

When You Are a Beggar…

You are free. You can go anywhere. Do anything. No one knows your name. Nobody—not even you—can remember when you were born, how old you are, or how you came to be here. You just are.

You can shit wherever, piss wherever, sleep everywhere and anywhere. You will eat anything. No matter how putrid, no matter how many mouths have bitten into that paratha in the trash can, you'll take it. You can wear anything; sometimes nothing at all. You could be lying naked under the seat of a jam-packed train and no one would even notice.

It is not easy to die when you are a beggar. Life clings to you like a rabid stray with its teeth sunken into your flesh. You manage to survive riots, floods, blackouts, morchas…And then you multiply. You father innumerable children with innumerable women who lie by the sides of the roads with their mouths and legs wide open. When you are a beggar you are always horny, always hungry. Ever-ready for one more fuck, one more morsel, one more rupee to buy one more speck of industrial-strength smack.

You discover that with time enough and a burning candle there is nothing that can't be coaxed into yielding its narcotic essence—rubber slippers, plastic bottles, wrappers, polished wood, coloured glass…The fumes are heavy and acrid. They swamp your lungs.

The resulting coma is deep, blank and absolute.

Days elapse in moments.

When you regain consciousness it could be afternoon or midnight and you could be anywhere—in a gutter, under a stationary train, or on the traffic island of Sion Junction. There is no telling how you got there. (There is no telling anything when you are a beggar.) You just get up and run. You scramble for the nearest shadowy corner where you are certain to find, huddled under filthy blankets, dirt-black people concocting the means to flee the world you have just re-entered. You don't speak to them; they don't even glance at you. The understanding is of a superior order. The chef is efficient; he is also just a twelve-year-old urchin. You wonder if he is your son. When he hands you a slit of foil with a drop of fuming battery acid, you want to kiss his hands.

And then you black out.

There is no pleasure in a beggar's high, no relief. It is black and airless, like being tied to the seabed. While your mind floats in ether, starvation drags your body around like a toy. The searing pain in your veins makes you run to and fro looking for something to burn and inhale. And always there is the ache of semen piling up every second, seeking release, seeking some soft moist crevice in which to spill itself—a dog, a chicken, a dead body…

Please, friend, money, food, hungry, God—these are the only words you need as a beggar; to charm the tourists, you learn to render these words in every tongue spoken under the sun.

Please, friend, money, food, hungry, God—soon, these are the only concepts you know, the only objects you recognize.

You start to believe that the solicitous is the only tone in which to address your fellow humans; that if you call people 'friend' they will be kind to you. You cannot think beyond the loose change in people's pockets. You cannot imagine being satiated by anything finer than food and sex.

And *God*?

Ha! That's just something you say to vex the indifferent fuckers.

Every twenty-nine days, a full moon quietly rises in the east. It is a silver that would take your breath away. When you are a beggar, you no longer have the words left to account for such extraordinary things.

Rahul Adhikari—Siddhartha in Denial

My Bombay is a cold, dry city.

I sleep under a blanket in my Bombay. (Preferably with someone who will go away before I get up, leaving strands of her hair on my pillow and traces of stale perfume on my sheets.)

On waking I turn on my cellphone. And then, sitting cross-legged at the edge of the bed, I try to meditate as demonstrated at last week's executive conference.

Walking through my penthouse after a scalding shower, I feel shivers in my lower ribs. It is freezing this morning. (But I will not lessen the air-conditioning.)

I microwave a cup of coffee. I sit at the kitchen counter with the newspaper—*Times of India*. There, there's your Bombay again, swamping my mind, bringing the whole of India with it. Before the clamour can mar my dignified morning, I chuck aside the chaos making news in your world.

I get ready. Here is what one wears to work in my Bombay: khakis, a woollen blazer and a cotton shirt.

The elevator is warm.

It takes me down.

The parking lot is sweltering!

Before my body can feel the shock, I dash through a wall of sunlit heat and leap into the back seat of my car, kept chilled and ready by Chinu, my driver, who has standing orders to arrive every morning by quarter to ten, fifteen minutes before I am to leave.

Everything happens on time in my Bombay.

Ten a.m. by my watch, but it seems like dusk outside. My car windows are practically black. If I moved my head a little to the right, I would see the blaze of the steaming, shitting, spitting city you live in. But I am not a romantic or a masochist, and even the windscreen is partially glazed to keep your Bombay out.

I stare down at my laptop while Chinu manipulates the Lancer through your streets. The car moves for some minutes, and halts for twice as much time.

Another fucking halt.

'Now what?' I ask Chinu.

'J.P. Road signal, sir.' He glances nervously in the rear-view mirror.

A shadow blocks the window on my left—the window I am seated at. The shadow begins tapping lightly from outside. I never look up or out. In my Bombay of incalculable bliss, one runs the risk of throwing it all away like an idiot at the first sight of suffering.

The tapping on the window increases—it becomes forceful; it sounds like a paw thumping against the glass.

Your Bombay wants a spare piece of mine.

'Give some change,' I order Chinu.

He depresses the button to lower the power window in the front-left. He stretches across and offers a five-rupee note through the narrow opening. The shadow outside rushes to the front. The note disappears. And, as the window goes up with a rubbery groan, Chinu shudders.

'Are you cold?' I ask. The air-conditioning is on High. But Chinu is wearing a sweater.

'No, sir. That beggar—looked like a corpse.' Chinu shudders again.

Ha. My driver lives in your Bombay. For him to be sickened must be an all-time low.

At eleven a.m., an hour later, we drive into the office complex. The car stops outside the main entrance.

I run into the glass-encased building—its cool lobby bathed in golden light, hawk-eyed security guards manning the reception desk.

My office is chilled and muted; it smells of ammonia and mothballs. Ducking past a volley of 'hi Rahul', 'morning Rahul', I sprint to my cabin.

At my desk, I slam my head down on the table and exhale with cheerless relief.

For one more day, for another twelve hours, I can, I must, I *will have to* forget that your Bombay exists.

*Bleep-bleep-bleep…bleep-bleep-bleep…*the direct line rings.

I raise my head. The caller ID shows an unknown number. I pick up the handset. 'Hello?'

'Let's just go this afternoon and get it done with,' a woman says.

'What?'

'There's no way out, okay!'

'*What?*'

'What do you mean *what*? Are you drunk?' the woman asks.

I slap my cheek to check if I am dreaming.

'Hello?' the woman says. 'Kasim, are you there?'

I fling the handset on the carpeted floor. 'IT'S THE WRONG NUMBER!' I yell at the receiver. 'HANG UP THE FREAKING PHONE! YOU HAVE THE WRONG FREAKING NUMBER!'

Kasim, the Right Number

It's inevitable. It has to be done. Our discussions, that have lasted through days and nights and right up to this morning, are over. The accusations, after being flung back and forth like parcels at a party, have finally ended up in both our hands: Minaz's and mine.

Attachment, fondness, respect, sexual attraction (yes, even that tyranny of the hormones) have all flown out the window.

'Kasim, let's just go this afternoon and get it done,' Minaz says.

After she hangs up the phone, my limbs turn to jelly. I remain on the bed; I find it impossible to move even a finger or swallow the saliva that starts to overflow from the side of my half-open mouth.

What Minaz and I are going to do this afternoon will wound us for ever—actually, her more than me, because for a man parenthood, or the rejection of it, remains an abstraction no matter how intense his emotions. Tonight, while she and I sleep in our respective bedrooms twelve kilometres apart, only one of our private parts will ache from the penetration of a surgical instrument, and it won't be my penis.

My penis!
That
bloody
bane
of an appendage

I pull down my shorts. I spot it amid the fuzz. It seems smaller than its usual flaccid length, like a crook cowering in court.

I grab my penis by its base, and with the other hand I begin slapping its soft, purple head. My organ jerks about. I shake it back and forth. I choke it till its brown skin reddens. And then I begin tugging at it and yanking it and squashing its head and plucking the hair at its base.

My eyes turn watery. A gasp escapes my lips as I twist my limp penis around my finger.

But I want more. More pain; more suffering. I want to ache the way I imagine Minaz will ache after the procedure is over and when the anaesthesia starts to wear off.

She will ache alone for something we did together.

So I torment my member in the hope that the agony will lessen my guilt.

But even that is not possible.

I am hopeless.

Despite the pain and the agony—and stimulated by the pinching, tweaking, twisting and slapping—my penis starts to turn hard.

'No!' I cry. 'No!'

I begin slapping both sides of my organ. I twist its swelling head. But the thing grows a life of its own; and no matter what I do to torture it, my organ continues to harden...

When the telephone rings again, fifteen minutes after Minaz had hung up, I am masturbating. Stroking my erect member, I am lost in an intricate fantasy comprising a composite of the women I've encountered over the past few days. Stupefied by lust, it takes me a few moments to even heed the ringing telephone.

I wipe my hand on my shorts and pick up the receiver.

It's Minaz again. Her voice sounds heavy, tremulous. 'You come to my place, we'll take my car,' she says. 'And hurry up, okay? The nursing home closes at three. Are you ready to leave?'

I have no answer.

In one hand is my erect penis. And in the other hand, pressed to my left ear, is a receiver transmitting the pained voice of a young girl who, willing as she was to sleep with me that afternoon several weeks ago, had no idea, as I did not, of the heavy price we'd have to pay for those few moments of pleasure.

'What are you doing? Why aren't you speaking?' Minaz cries.

'I'll...I was about to leave...I'll be there soon.' I put down the receiver.

How?

As I stare at my penis—which has begun to wilt in the absence of friction—my eyes widen, my jaw drops and a spit bubble pops in my mouth.

Hours before my lover and I are to abort our unborn embryo, I am keeping her waiting in order to enjoy one more sad, solitary *orgasm*?

I am sick.

I can't be trusted any more.

I should be exiled to the forest.

What do I know!

Nothing.

I'm a monkey!

I know nothing!

I rise from the bed and pull up my shorts. The skin of my semi-hard member burns on contact with cloth.

I stand in the middle of the room.

My eyes are smarting. I am shaking my head in disbelief. How? How did I progress from torturing my penis to pleasuring it? And that too on a morning like *this*?

Ten more minutes pass.

The landline starts to ring.

I remain motionless.

After seven rings, it goes silent.

My cellphone rings: a tinny, digitally simplified version of the national anthem. I lower myself to the floor—very slowly, like the world is resting on my shoulders. I extricate the gadget from under the bed sheet.

It's Minaz again. 'Have you left home already?' she asks.

I lie. 'Yes.'

There's a quizzical silence at the other end. 'Why do *you* sound so down?' she says. 'I should be sounding sad, not you. This doesn't even affect you.'

Such bitterness already.

'Minaz…I'm…I'm really sorry…'

It is my first apology since learning of her pregnancy two weeks ago. It is unforgivably late. But at least it is genuine.

She turns incoherent: 'HOW… FUCK YOU… HOW DARE YOU, YOU FUCKING…DON'T FUCK AROUND WITH MY HEAD, KASIM… I… KEEP YOUR SORRYS TO YOURSELF… JUST COME WITH ME TODAY… I DON'T WANT… I JUST WANT TO GET RID…'

Her shouts turn into shrieks.

She disconnects the phone.

It starts from the liver. A quiver that ripples through my torso. Soon my whole body is trembling.

I am a hazard.

I am a bloody fool. Minaz is probably right. This is all my fault. Even though we used a condom, even though we were careful to the point of lunacy, somehow something went wrong, and it was most certainly I who caused it.

I get dressed without bathing.

I leave home unseen by my family and come down to the crowded street. The air is boiling in the mid-morning sun.

I start walking towards the closest bus stop.

Terrified of causing any more harm, of making any more mistakes, I move v-e-r-y carefully through the mob of pedestrians. I walk like a soldier in enemy territory. I keep my eyes open, ears tuned and breath steady.

My cellphone rings again. The caller ID shows Zubin, a college mate. I reject the call. No more friends, no more distractions, no more GMAT scores, vital stats, passwords, lyrics or dialogues crowding my brain like snot.

From now on I must try to have as little to do with the world as possible. It's the only way I can protect others from myself. From now on, I must keep close track of every single breath.

There is a huge crowd at the bus stop.

The 95 arrives. Men, women and children rush forward. I am shoved to the side. I find myself at the back of the crowd. I board the bus at the very last, when the conductor rings the bell and as the bus starts to move.

With a foot on the boarding platform and a hand clutching the metal railing, I'm on the 95, but only just.

It's the way I intend to live my life from now—on the periphery.

Tethered, but only just.

I stand through the forty-five-minute journey.

I get off at Agripada and walk to the gate of Ismat Towers. I send a text message to Minaz telling her I'm here. I wait for five minutes. No reply. I dial her cellphone. She doesn't answer. The watchman knows me and allows me in.

I enter the elevator and press 16, the top floor. The metal doors rumble close. My ears pop as the elevator ascends.

The air feels thinner on the sixteenth floor. There is a hushed silence in the sunlit lobby.

I ring the bell of flat 1602. The wooden door has geometric designs carved into it, and at its centre is a rust iron nameplate that says:

KHWAJAS

Twenty minutes later, Minaz is driving us to Colaba. She insists she is perfectly capable, even on a day like this, of manoeuvring her Wagon-R through the city's treacherous traffic. We're strapped down in our seats, our faces chilled by the conditioned air blasting from the vents on the dashboard. Her parents assumed I had come to collect their daughter for yet another harmless day out. Minaz is honking too much; she is beeping at anything that moves on the road. I glance at her repeatedly. She once claimed her left profile was more flattering. Right now I doubt she cares what angle I see her from. We are not talking. There is nothing left to say. We are driving past VT towards Fountain. Colaba is ten minutes away. We are not sentimental fools. Neither of us wants to become a parent like this—under duress, with regret. Besides, after this morning, I know how unprepared I am for fatherhood. 'You brought your license?' Minaz asks, with an eye on the rear-view mirror. 'Yes,' I say. I will be driving us back to Agripada from the nursing home. There is an inferno in my underwear; I have only now begun to realize to what extent I had injured my penis. And there is gratitude—a shameful and hopeless gratitude towards Minaz for consenting to the desecration of her body in order to salvage our shining futures.

We reach Colaba and park the car near the post office. Minaz and I start walking towards Pasta Lane. Someone seems to be holding a magnifying glass over the city this afternoon. The sun's heat has never been this intense, this punishing.

Love is known to strengthen after a single shared event of intolerable grief—a partner's infidelity, the demise of a child. I suppose it's the price people have to pay to remain together. Minaz and I have been together for eight fun-filled, giddy-headed months. After this afternoon, after we have paid our price, I suppose she and I will become inseparable.

'We're here,' she says and starts to enter Shamma Nursing Home. I don't follow her in. I want to hug her. But I don't want to offend her.

Minaz comes out to the footpath and gives me her trademark tough stare—the look that has no one fooled.

'Okay?' I ask. She snorts.

We step into the dimly lit waiting room. Minaz's heartbeats

are hitting me like sonic booms.

A man is standing with his back to us. He is gazing at the frosted pane of a closed window. There is no one else in here. Distracted by our entry, he turns to look at us.

Is he?

Could this be?

No.

No. Clearly not.

This can't be the doctor. This man is wearing a striped shirt and black pants. There is nothing remarkable about him—no tortured eyes, no dark circles or blotchy skin, nothing to indicate that he is the doer of the deed that Minaz and I have been agonizing over day and night for the past three weeks. This man looks like a shopkeeper.

I ask, 'You…you are the doctor?'

I am half-expecting a shorter, fatter, darker and older individual to sneak out from the adjoining room and announce in a coarse, phlegmatic voice, 'No, I am the doctor.'

I lose my bearings when the man in the striped shirt nods to indicate that he is, in fact, the doctor. That he is, in fact, the nadir of our lives. That he is, in fact, the abortionist.

*Everybody, sooner or later, sits down to
a banquet of consequences.*

Robert Louis Stevenson

Read more in Penguin

MAXIMUM CITY: BOMBAY LOST AND FOUND
Suketu Mehta

'A gripping, compellingly readable account of a love affair with a city: I couldn't put it down.'—Amitav Ghosh

Suketu Mehta left Bombay at the age of fourteen. Twenty-one years later, having lived in Paris, London and New York's East Village, he returned to rediscover the only city he calls his own. The result is this stunning, brilliantly illuminating portrait of the megalopolis and its people.

Mehta approaches the life and lives of Bombay from unexpected angles. He takes us into the underworld where Muslim and Hindu gangs manage to wrest some control of the Byzantine political and commercial systems of the city. He follows the life of a bar dancer, whose childhood of poverty and abuse left her no choice but the one she made. He journeys on the famed local trains and out onto the streets and footpaths, where the essential story of Bombay is played out every day by the countless migrants who come in search of a better life. And through it all—as each individual story unfolds—we hear Mehta's own story: of the mixture of love, frustration, fascination, and intense identification he feels for and with Bombay.

Candid, impassioned, insightful, both surprisingly funny and heart-rending, *Maximum City* is a revelation of a complex and ever-changing world: the continent of Bombay.

Non-fiction
India Rs 595

Read more in Penguin

SADAK CHHAAP
Meher Pestonji

'How was he to know where he belonged? . . . Was he to accept street life as his destiny?'

The day ten-year-old Rahul, part-time rag-picker, pickpocket and petty thief living footloose on the streets of Bombay, finds an abandoned baby on a railway platform, his life changes forever.

He quickly appoints himself the baby's father, making her the emotional anchor that had been missing from his life. And, while he is treated as quite the hero within his street community, he wins the trust and affection of people who are willing to give him the opportunity to start afresh and work towards a better future.

But the streets are mean, inescapable, and as Rahul indulges his paltry desires and shallow dreams, he finds himself spiralling, yet again, into a vortex of crime, abuse and loneliness.

As horrific as it is heartbreaking, *Sadak Chhaap* evokes the brutal existence of street urchins with unrelenting realism and deep sympathy.

Fiction
India Rs 250